Storytellers

Tales of Hope, Humour and Heartbreak

by

David R. Grigg

Illustrated by Robert Brunton OAM

Published by Rightword Enterprises

ISBN: 978-0-9872654-2-5
2nd Edition

A publication of Rightword Enterprises:
www.rightword.com.au

*Cover design by the author, based on an image licensed from
CanStockPhoto.com*

For Kathryn, who listened to my stories

.

Contents

The Kid

Benny James was proud of his skills. He'd been practising and improving them for nearly ten years, ever since he had started out at the age of fourteen. He'd had to keep changing and improvising all the time since. He was in a race against technology, like an arms race, he thought. The manufacturers kept coming up with new ways to defeat him. He had to keep on coming up with ways to beat them.

Benny stole cars for a living.

Today he was looking out for a particular brand and model. That wasn't usual, but Jason Baxter had asked him to lift one, had a client who wanted just that type of car. Benny didn't much care the reason, so long as he got his cut.

Anyway, he'd been hanging about the petrol station for nearly an hour. It was early morning, just after the peak hour. Benny always made sure there wouldn't be too much traffic, so that he could make a quick getaway.

The problem with a modern car like the one Jason wanted was that it had too many fancy anti-theft gadgets. With a car like that, you couldn't just quickly hot-wire it in the dead of night. You could get around the gadgets with enough time, but the simplest way was just to get hold of the keys. If you were as sharp and as nippy as Benny, it wasn't too hard to do that.

Finally, the right kind of car pulled up to a bowser. Even better, there was a woman driver. Women were better targets all round, not so much because they wouldn't put up a fight -- Benny was short and skinny and had no intention of getting into a fight -- but because they were often encumbered by handbags and other junk.

He sidled closer as the woman got out of the car and went around to the bowser. He smiled inwardly as he saw her place her keys on the flat boot of the car in order to better manage the pump. Perfect. Benny would have knocked the keys out of her hand if he'd had to -- people generally held them loosely -- but this was far easier.

He sprinted, snatched the keys off the boot, leapt into the driver's seat and was screeching into the street before the woman had even begun to scream.

While staying just within the speed limit, he drove as fast as he could, twisting around several corners, just squeaking through a few intersections on the orange light. He knew this part of town perfectly, lived here all his life, could have driven the route blindfold. He flicked a glance down at the fuel gauge. The only problem with nicking a car this way was that the fuel was bound to be low. He'd done one job where the damned car had run out of gas in the next block, and he'd had to dump it and run. But there was easily enough in this one. He wasn't going far.

Round two more corners, down a narrow back alley, through the rickety wooden gates he'd left open that morning, and into the carport.

Only then did he look into the mirror to check that no-one was following him down the alley.

There was a face staring back at him.

Benny literally jumped with shock. "Fuck!"

It was a kid, eyes wide open in fascination, strapped into one of those child restraints.

Benny groaned, panic rising. "Oh fuck, fuck, fuck! You're not supposed to be there. Geez, geez, what am I gonna do with you?"

Benny jumped out of the car, literally hopped with agitation as he rushed to close the gates to his back yard to conceal the car from view. It wasn't much of a yard, filled as it was with the carport and an aging diseased lemon tree, dropping its scabby fruit. Moira called it their 'back half-yard'.

Moira. Moira would know what to do. *Ah, shit*, he thought. Moira would skin him alive, that's what she'd do.

Benny stared at the kid, who was sitting calmly in the child seat, looking around with interest at these new surroundings, but clinging on tightly to a small teddy bear. Benny couldn't think what the hell to do with the kid. He could hardly just drive the car back to the gas station, hand over the kid and apologise. He'd be in jail so fast he wouldn't see the door close.

He wasn't sure how old this kid was. Benny didn't have much experience with children. This one seemed too young to be talking. At least, it wasn't *doing* any talking. But as he watched, the kid's lower lip started to tremble. *Shit, it's going to start bawling,* he thought, *and all the neighbours will hear.*

Making what he hoped were calming noises, he fumbled the kid out of the restraint. God, there were so many damned straps and connectors! "Hush now, hush, hush," Benny kept on repeating. Finally he could lift the kid up into his arms, and staggered with it through the back door of their rented house, one of several in the terrace block. Geez, the kid was heavy.

Inside the kitchen, with the door closed safely behind him, he gratefully set the kid down on the floor. It seemed perfectly happy to stand, and indeed started to totter around the kitchen investigating things, just like a curious kitten, still clutching its bear. The kid had a somewhat bow-legged gait due to its bulky pants. A nappy, Benny supposed vaguely.

Benny stood looking at the wandering child, still completely at sea as to what to do. He might be a small-time crook, but he didn't think of himself as a bad person. And he certainly didn't mean the kid any harm. He stared at it in a kind of daze.

The kid started to grizzle, and repeatedly put its finger into its mouth. *Maybe it's hungry,* Benny thought, and desperately looked around. There might be some milk in the fridge, he thought, but would he have to put it into a bottle? Then he spotted a banana in the fruit bowl. Moira did all the shopping of course, tried to make sure they ate right.

Benny peeled the banana and the kid looked up and clapped its little hands. It grabbed the fruit as

Benny proffered it, and started to scarf it down while still tottering around the kitchen.

Benny glanced at the clock. Moira would be home in a couple of hours. She only worked mornings on a Wednesday. What the fuck was he going to tell her? God, he needed a joint.

Somehow he shepherded the kid into the tiny lounge room. There were too many sharp things in the kitchen. He sank down gratefully on the couch, and the kid managed to clamber up next to him. After a while, it started to yawn and rub its little eyes with tiny fists. Seizing this opportunity, Benny picked the kid up again and took it into the bedroom. He laid it down on the double bed and folded a corner of the quilt over it. The kid seemed to be content, hugging its little teddy bear, and was soon soundly asleep.

Profoundly grateful, Benny went back to the lounge room and hunted up his stash. Rolling himself a joint, he lit up. When he'd smoked it down to the last stub, feeling much more content and now hardly worried at all, he settled back on the couch and drifted off into a snooze.

He was woken abruptly some time later by Moira's heavy hand.

"Benny, you good-for-nothing little twerp, what in God's holy name have you been doing? There's a child in our bed!" Moira was Irish, and red-headed with it.

Benny was still high, though coming down from it quickly, and he desperately floundered around for an excuse. "Ah, err, it's my sister's kid. She asked me to look after it for a bit."

"And why in God's high heaven would she be so stupid as to ask a deadbeat like you to look after her baby?"

"Well, err, there was a family emergency."

"It must have been. Ah, there now, it's awake and crying, the wee thing." She hurried off to the bedroom. Only a moment later she popped her head back. "It's sopping wet, Benny. Did you not think to change its nappy?" He shook his head silently, still trying to come down from his high.

"So where's the bag, then?" Moira called from the bedroom.

"Bag? What bag?"

"Mother Mary save me! Did your sister not give you a bag with clean nappies and things in it?"

"Err, no. No. Like I said, it was kind of an emergency."

"Oh well, then, I'll have to improvise with a hand towel or something."

There was a long silence and then Moira's voice came again. This time it had a dangerous, threatening tone. "Benny..."

She came out, holding the kid, which seemed quite content, its thumb in its mouth.

"Benny," said Moira flatly. "Did you not get me to buy your sister's bubby a jump-suit when it was born? A *pink* jump-suit, Benny? Not a *blue* jump-suit,

Benny. A *pink* jump-suit. For a *girl*, Benny?" And she held up the child, now naked from the waist down. It was clearly *not* a little girl.

So he had to tell her the truth.

"Holy Mary, Mother of God!" she said, her eyes flaming. "You stupid idiot! Imagine what this poor child's mother is going through right now. She'll be frantic. And the police will be all over it. Kidnapping, that's what it will be. You bloody fool, they'll thump you into a dark hole and leave you there until you rot!"

Benny winced from her fury. "I didn't mean to snatch the kid, it was just a mistake, I was just nicking a car for Jason."

"*Just?!* You lazy bastard, if you'd only get yourself a real job this kind of thing wouldn't happen. Ah, Christ, what's the use?" She stood silent for a moment. "Here, you hold the kid for a bit. I hope he widdles on you. Give me the keys to the damned car, I'll bet the mother has a baby bag in there."

Benny awkwardly held the kid out away from him, aiming it away just in case. After a minute or two Moira returned, carrying a bulky blue bag. "Give him to me," she said curtly, and took the child off, to return after a while with it fully clothed again. She went off to the kitchen with it and when she returned the kid was sipping from a small cup of milk.

"Now," she said. "What are we going to do with this poor child?"

Benny shuffled his feet. "Err, I dunno. Maybe we could sell it?"

She was volcanic in her fury. "Jesus Christ and all his saints! If you ever even *think* something like that again, Benny, I'll get the kitchen knife and I'll cut off your balls! And that will just be the start. What I *meant* was, how are we going to get this child back to its sorrowing mother, you little tick."

"I can't just take it back, Moira. Like you said, they'll throw me in the clink as soon as look at me."

She shook her head in anger. "Unless we can come up with another idea in less than ten minutes, Benny, that's exactly what you're going to do. Either that, or I'll march this child into the nearest police station and I'll shop you, Benny, I swear to God I will." She put the child down. It happily wandered off around the lounge. Benny hastily picked up his stash and hid it away again. Moira, meanwhile, was investigating the blue bag. There was a smaller bag inside with clean clothes in it. This one had printing all over it, advertising a child-care centre.

"OK," she said. "I've got a plan." She thought for a couple more minutes. "All right," she said. "This is it. I'm going to drive the kid to this child care centre, it's not far away. In the car you stole. It will be risky... unless... Benny have you got a set of spare number plates? Come on, I know you have. Get out there and switch the plates on the stolen car. Bring the ones you take off back to me. Then we're going to drive, in a little convoy, you and me. I'll be in the car you stole. You'll be in my car, following."

"But Jason is expecting..."

"Fuck Jason and fuck you too. This is how it's going to be, Benny. You'll follow me in my car, we'll leave the mother's car there at the centre, and Jason can just stuff it."

It worked out as Moira planned. She pulled over at the child care centre in the stolen car with its switched plates. It was late afternoon by now, and there were plenty of mothers, and some fathers too, picking up their kids. Plenty of them had other kids in tow, so it didn't seem at all out of place for Moira to be carrying a child into the centre. Benny watched, sitting in Moira's car with the engine running. Just as she went in, he saw the kid look back and give him a cheerful wave.

Moments later, Moira came running out of the centre and leapt into the car. "Go, go, go!" she yelled, out of breath.

Benny drove quickly away. "It went all right, then?"

"Sure. Those places are designed to make it hard for someone to snatch a child and take it out of the centre, not to stop you bringing in an extra one. I just plonked the kid in behind the barrier, dumped the bag on the counter, and then slapped down the original number plates with a bang. They'll call the cops, sure as eggs. I think it's all OK."

Then she gripped him hard on the shoulder, so hard that he winced and wobbled the car a bit.

"But Benny, my stupid, stupid love. After this you get yourself off the dope and you go straight, straight as a die, straight as a ruler, and you go get yourself an honest job. Because, Benny, if you don't, I swear I'll shop you to the police for this, so help me God I will."

He didn't hesitate for a moment. "Yes, Moira," he said meekly.

The Other Car

Sergeant Jacobs heaved his massive bulk out of the squad car. Constable Evans got out of the driver's side, eyeing his superior with a degree of disgust. *Time the old bastard gave it away*, he thought. Always a big man, Jacobs had added a hefty beer-gut in recent years, the legacy of decades of heavy drinking.

Evans glanced around at the yard around the farmhouse. It was decrepit, a total mess. An out-building near the gate where they had parked the car was in the process of a very slow-motion collapse, one wall leaning over drunkenly and the corrugated iron of its roof rusted and half sliding off. Chickens ran here and there, gabbling, eyed by a grey-haired old dog lying in the shade of an ancient lemon tree. The dog looked as if it had just collapsed there from exhaustion. It was surrounded by rotting lemons, visited by evil-looking European wasps.

"Christ!" said Jacobs. "Been a bloody long time since this place was a goer. D'ya see how overgrown the paddocks are? The neighbours must be ropeable. Bloody fire hazard." He stared around in disgust, then signalled to Evans. "Come on, kid, let's see what the old bloke has to say."

It was a hot, hot day, the middle of January. Bush-fire season. The air was full of the sound of scream-ing cicadas. Evans looked back at the long dry grass in the paddocks and thought that Sergeant Jacobs was right. The neighbours would be furious that the farmer here had let them get that way. One spark, and the whole place would go up and spread in minutes to the neighbouring properties.

But it might all be part of the same story. Bill Greaves, the owner here, was in pretty deep shit by the sound of it.

Jacobs led the way across the yard, and onto the veranda of the farmhouse. The wooden floor of the veranda was an obstacle course, with several broken boards, on top of support beams which had also seen better days. Evans followed gingerly.

Jacobs hammered on the door. No answer, though Evans thought he heard a grunt or a snort from inside.

There was a bell hanging up outside, like a school bell or a dinner bell. Jacobs took it off the hook and rang it vigorously. "Greaves?" he yelled. "Where are ya? Police!" He rang the bell again. "Bill Greaves! Get out here!"

There was a groan and a series of muttered curses from inside, and Evans heard stumbling, something being knocked over, more curses. Finally, a bleary-eyed man staggered to the door. "What d'ya want?"

Bill Greaves looked to be in his mid seventies, tall, with a mess of dirty white hair that ran from his head down into the stubble of his beard. His shirt was filthy, and he seemed to have lost his belt, because his trousers sagged around his hips. He'd once been a strong, powerful man, Evans thought, but now he looked like only a shadow of that.

"What the fuck d'ya want?" he repeated weakly. He was drunk, of course. But Evans sensed a deeper confusion there, too. Despite the swearing, there was no aggression in the old man. Instead, there was just fear and bafflement.

"Can we see Mrs Greaves, Bill? Where's Mary?" said the sergeant. That was why they had come. No one in the nearby town had seen Greaves' wife in the last three months. Though the couple had always kept to themselves, Mrs Greaves would visit the town to shop at least once every few weeks, buy the groceries, maybe get her hair done once in a while. It had taken the townsfolk a long while to realize that she seemed to have stopped coming, and then to do something about it.

Greaves supported himself on the door frame. "No, no," he mumbled. "She's not here right now. Gone into town."

"She's not in the town, Bill. How would she get there? Your car's in the driveway, there." As indeed it was, a battered old Ford Falcoln.

"The other car, she took our other car. The other car." Greaves was looking desperately about, his eyes flicking back and forth. With a sickening feeling, Constable Evans realized he could smell something bad wafting out of the house. He hadn't smelled – hadn't seen – a dead body yet in his short career. Could this be what it smelled like?

"Your other car," said Jacobs sarcastically. "That'd be the Merc, would it? Or is it a Roller? Didn't know you was so well off, Bill."

Greaves had missed the sarcasm, though, and was nodding vigorously. "Yeah, yeah, the other car."

"You'd better let us in, Bill," said Jacobs, unceremonially pushing his way past Greaves into the house. Jacobs wasn't much on formal procedure, but Evans knew he would have to write it up afterwards as if they had formally requested permission and waited for acceptance. Greaves stumbled after him, and Jacobs waved at him to sit down on a couch. Greaves sat down like a collapsing house of cards.

Jacobs nodded to Evans. "Why don't you go for a little walk, Constable? Find out where the loo is. I might want a piss in a minute."

Evans unhappily took the broad hint and went off to look through the house. The awful smell was worse in here, and he had a leaden feeling in his stomach. There wasn't much to the house, the living room where Jacobs was talking to Greaves, a couple of bedrooms, one full of junk, the other with an unmade bed and sheets the colour of coffee, which Evans didn't think was the colour the manufacturer had intended. A bathroom. No toilet, that would be outside. And the kitchen, which proved to be the source of the disgusting smell.

The smell was coming from the old Kelvinator fridge. Evans felt a tremor inside. Could it be? Damn, he'd seen too many horror movies. *Pull yourself together*, he thought savagely.

He hesitated for a moment before opening the fridge, then looked around. He flicked on the room light. Nothing. No power. They were on town electricity here, he knew. Maybe Greaves had stopped paying his bills and it had been cut off. Or maybe it was just a blown fuse or two.

Taking a deep breath, he opened the fridge. Gagging, he stared at ranks of mouldy, decaying food. He opened the freezer compartment, and nearly threw up. A huge chunk of stinking, rotting meat. Was that, had it been...? No. It was just a leg of lamb, now a curious shade of green.

Evans closed the fridge door and left the kitchen in relief. He wasn't sure what Greaves had been eating for the last few weeks, but it hadn't been anything out of that fridge. Veggies from his garden and the odd chook, he supposed. He found his way back to Sergeant Jacobs and Bill Greaves.

Jacobs was saying, "So how long has she been gone, Bill? When did she leave? In your other car?" He glanced up at Evans, who shook his head mutely.

Greaves was sitting on a saggy old couch which was half covered in dog hair. For the moment he seemed to have inexplicably cheered up, was now almost chatty. "Oh, been a while now, quite a while. She should be back soon, though. Soon. Gone to get me some more beer. Took the other car. Couldn't start the Falcoln." He looked around vaguely. Empty beer bottles littered the floor, and there was a half-empty bottle of what looked like cooking sherry on the side table next to the couch. "Need some more beer."

"Christ, you wouldn't want to put it in that fridge," muttered Evans.

Jacobs looked at Evans, frowning. "She's not in the house?" he confirmed. "No?" He turned back to Greaves. "See here, Bill. Mary's not here, and she's not in the town. Where is she? No bullshitting, now. Where's she gone?"

Greaves sat there staring for a long, long moment, his mouth wide open. He can't just be drunk, Evans thought. There's more to his confusion than that. Alzheimer's, probably. His old grandma had gone gaga like that, towards the end. Mind you, the alcohol wasn't helping matters.

Suddenly, it seemed, Greaves' foggy brain cleared a little and he looked up with a confused frown and a down-turned mouth, his momentary cheerfulness gone. "No, no. Not beer. She was feeling crook, I remember now. Feeling crook, so I drove her into town, drove her in to the hospital. That's where she is, at the hospital!" He looked up in pathetic triumph.

"No, Bill," said Jacobs, almost tenderly. "She's not in the hospital. Come on, now, you need to remember."

But Greaves was insistent. "No, no, I took her in the other car. In the ute. Falcoln wouldn't start, fucking thing. Fucking thing!" He was yelling now. "Fucking thing wouldn't start. Not fair!" He quietened. "So I took her in the other car. She was crook, had to carry her." He stopped suddenly and shook his head. "No, no, no. No. Not the car."

Jacobs looked speculatively at Evans. "Not the car. Didn't think so."

"No," said Greaves. "Got rid of that car. Bought a Chevy. Not a car. A ute. Yanks call it a truck, but it's a ute. Beaut ute," he added, laughing drunkenly at his own joke. "I took her in the ute."

"And where is this ute, Bill? You drove Mary in to the hospital, you say. You must have driven yourself back. Where's the ute?"

For a moment Greaves' face showed a renewed confusion. Then he seemed to regain his memory and he suddenly slapped his palm against his leg. "It's out the back, we always keep the other car out the back. Come on, I'll show you. It's a beaut ute."

He staggered to his feet and wobbled toward the back door. The two policemen followed him.

The back yard was, if anything, worse than the front. Young wattle trees grew up where once there might have been a vegetable patch, and more massive gums thrust up through the line of a fence.

And there, half hidden by the foliage, was Bill Greaves' other car. His beaut ute.

It hadn't been driven in decades. It was half rust now, its tires long rotted away, its engine dismantled, grass growing in patches on the deck of the tray. And in the passenger seat, almost hidden by a mass of buzzing bushflies, was Mary Greaves.

Long Exposure

It had been a great deal of effort, and she had needed a lot of help, but the exhibition was open at last. 'A Retrospective Exhibition of the Work of Howard James Carver'. Funny that she'd never known about the 'James'. Or perhaps that wasn't funny at all.

When she had first been told of her legacy in Carver's will, Pauline had at first been astonished, and then quite angry. What a responsibility, what a burden, to be left with! She hadn't even *seen* the man for more than twenty years.

But she knew that his only marriage had fallen apart in a bitter divorce a few years ago, and there hadn't been any children. Maybe after all it wasn't too surprising that he'd thought of her when writing his will. The bastard could have left her some money, though. Instead, it had been his photographic legacy, every image he'd taken in forty-odd years, with all of the reproduction rights.

That sounded romantic enough, and eventually it might earn her some money, but the world had moved on from Carver — he hadn't been able to make a successful transition from film to digital — and in practice his legacy to her had been a dusty room lined with shelves and packed with box after box of prints and negatives.

Thank heavens the State Art Gallery had been helpful, had been able to get some money from the government to stage this exhibition. Pauline would never have been able to cope with sorting through all of Howard Carver's prints by herself, but the Gallery's curators had been wonderful. And they had been willing to accept Carver's photographs into their permanent collection, while leaving her a percentage of the reproduction rights.

So now it was the evening before the three-week exhibition was to open. Later that night, a reporter was coming from the local newspaper, and Pauline was expected to walk around with her and talk about the photographs that had been selected for display, talk about their history.

Arming herself for that task now, Pauline walked slowly around the exhibition by herself, looking at each image in turn.

Here were the earliest years. She and Howard had been students at the Tech, doing the same Photography course. Displayed here was some of his early work, done for course projects. These images were now notable mostly for historical reasons, though several did show the promise of the remarkable talent he was later to demonstrate.

To her, they were memorable for the shared intimacy they had had in the darkroom, bathed in that deep red light, she placing the photographic paper and he turning on the projector, then dodging some of the areas with a little lolly-pop hade to stop them over-exposing. How different it all was now in the digital era with such things as HDR!

Their intimacy, of course, had quickly extended to the bedroom. Their first night together, he had climbed up and replaced his normal room light with a red globe. She could have taken that the wrong way, but instead she'd laughed, and they had made awkward but ultimately satisfying love in the ruddy glow.

Here on the gallery wall now were the inevitable nude photographs of her own body. She gave a little sigh for the long-lost perfection of the shapes she saw here.

She'd been strangely prudish for the '60s, at least compared with how people nowadays thought of the '60s, and had always insisted that these photographs never showed her face. She had been worried that her parents might somehow see them, she supposed. So these images were classic black-and-white artistic nudes, their focus on the ideal female form, the smooth curves, the rises and shallows. How perfect her skin had been then, how free from blemish and wrinkle!

Here on the gallery wall now was one of those images she remembered best — the perfect twin domes of her buttocks. She smiled, remembering how he had had to keep cranking up the heat in the studio until she lost her goosebumps.

She walked on. A long, long series now followed of herself in various poses, in various settings, in various lighting, in various clothes. Howard had called her his muse, used her as a model all of the time, almost obsessively. She had started to resent it quite early on.

Howard was enamoured of black and white photography, and remained so throughout his life. But her own interests had started to move in the direction of colour and towards nature photography. His incessant demands for her to model for him in the studio had started to interfere annoyingly with her own desire for trips into the wild, and with her time to process and mount her work.

There had been arguments. "You're only interested in seeing me at the other end of a camera lens!" she had yelled at him one day, and although he vehemently denied it, proclaimed his eternal love, made passionate love to her, she knew that it was becoming true.

She had continued to be fascinated by his work, though, and had continued to model for him despite her irritation. But his work had started to change.

It was all clearly laid out on the gallery wall. She'd been surprised, as she and the curators had chosen the pictures over the last few weeks, about how obvious it was. It hadn't seemed so at the time.

The photos told the story as she walked past them in chronological order. They moved from close-ups of her face, to head-and-shoulders portraits, to full-figure shots framed in doorways and arches.

As time — and their arguments — went on, he had told her that he wanted to get out of the studio more, had started to become interested in the human figure in the landscape. The images that resulted had her perching on a rock, or framed between two huge trees, or sitting in profile overlooking a harbour.

She had enjoyed these outdoor expeditions, had used the opportunity to develop her macro skills, photographing sunlit dew on a leaf, a raindrop half-swallowing a bright red beetle.

Howard, on the other hand, started to use wider and wider lenses, capturing more and more of her surrounds and less of her, though he still insisted, *insisted* that she be in his images. "It's you I'm shooting," he always said.

Here now were a set of prints of her on that cold beach in Normandy. God, it had been cold that day! There was actually snow in patches on the sand. She'd been rugged up, hardly an attractive figure, carrying her big bag, but he had found a perfect set of sand dunes, and photographed her from a distance, silhouetted against a bright sky. She'd laughed when she saw the print — her figure seemed to be balanced on two huge buttocks — the perfect companion to that nude image of her body from years before.

Then the final series. He'd taken her to that town in Czechoslovakia, what was it called? Prague had been too busy, he'd said, too full of people.

He was experimenting, taking long exposure shots with a dense neutral filter over the lens. Early one morning, before most people were up, he'd made her stand in the centre of a cobbled street in the middle distance. He did one or two shots, then moved the camera back half a block. And again, and

again, his shouted instructions eventually just becoming distant semaphore.

Here were the prints now on the wall.

The long exposures had blurred out the move-
ment of any people or vehicles which had been up
and about at that early hour. Except for herself,
standing, at his instructions, rock-still. The effect was
like that image she had seen from the earliest days of
photography, when exposures had by necessity to be
minutes-long, in which the only human figure visible in a Paris street had been a many who stood still
while his shoes were shined.

And now here was the very last image of her in
the gallery. A long, long, cobbled street. A tiny figure
in the far distance, all by herself.

Even before she had seen the print, she had
known that it was time to leave him.

Murder Ballads

"You're taking me *where*? Oh, God, I *hate* folk music! And you've got a freaking *guitar* strung over your back? Michael, you look like a goddamn hippy!"

His heart sank. This was not a promising start.

It was only their third date. Well, two-and-a-halfth, maybe. The first had really just come about by chance when they found themselves at the same table in the canteen, and spent a glorious hour bitching about their physics professor. He'd fallen for her then, in a big way. He loved her dark eyes, her slender neck. And her *passion* – her family were Italian. He found that he couldn't take his eyes off her.

Then they'd had dinner together at the cheap Vietnamese noodle shop he knew. They had discovered a mutual interest in Terry Pratchett's books, and had spent the time yelling over the hubbub at each other about their favourite characters.

Somehow the subject of music hadn't come up until now. Stupidly, he'd thought to surprise her. Well, he'd done that all right.

They were still walking together down the street towards the club. At least she hadn't stormed off, that was something.

"Why do you hate it?" he managed. "Traditional music is important. Well, that is, I like it," he finished clumsily.

"Oh, I don't mind the *melodies*. Some great tunes. It's just the awful *lyrics*. All folk songs are about someone dying, or getting killed, or being murdered. Murder ballads, isn't that what someone called them?"

"Nick Cave," he said bitterly. "Or at least he put an album out called that."

Despair was weighing on him. He really, really liked Claudia, had had high hopes. But this was a little like being a Christian and then finding out that your date was a militant atheist. Or that you loved meat and she was a vegan. It was the end of everything.

Desperately, he rallied. "Not all folk songs are like that, not at all. And anyway, there's a lot of dying in most love stories – Romeo and Juliet, Tristan and…"

"Isolde, yes." Now she shifted ground, a dangerous sign. "And they all treat women as pathetic *objects*, always being carted off against their will, or having their fathers or their husbands kill their lovers. Either that, or they are killed themselves for being unfaithful. *Mamma Mia!*" She added the last just for effect, she spoke hardly any Italian.

"It's not all like that," he said stubbornly. "Anyway, what kind of music do *you* like?", he asked, hoping to find common ground.

Surprisingly, she seemed slightly abashed, took a moment to answer. "Well… Modern classical, I guess you'd call it. Arvo Pärt, John Tavener. Philip Glass?" She added the last looking up at him with a slight frown. "You must have heard of Philip Glass?"

Hope edged back in him. It seemed as though she did want to find some agreement, too.

"Philip Glass... I saw that film with the funny name, what was it called? Ky... Kow..."

"*Koyaanisqatsi*," she finished promptly. "Did you like the music in *that*?" she asked eagerly.

"Um, well, I liked the film, but I don't really remember the music, much. Except for the bit at the start, with the guy with the really deep voice, saying Koy... that word.. Over and over again."

"Oh, *Michael*!" She literally stopped and stamped her foot. Half of him observed this with curiosity, he'd never actually seen someone do that in reality.

She glared up at him. "What about *The Hours*?"

"Was that the film where Nicole Kidman.... "

"...won the Oscar for playing Virginia Woolf. With a false nose. Yes. Did you see that?"

"No."

She threw up her hands in disgust.

They were at the club now, and hesitated at the door. "Come on in," he said. "It's not a commercial club, or anything, it's just a few of us, half a dozen, and we each just sing one or two songs. Give it a try. I'll sing you a folk song that's not like the ones you were talking about."

She thought it over. Slowly. Michael mentally had his fingers crossed, hoping.

"Oh, what the hell. Let's do it." And they went in.

Unfortunately, the first few songs the others sang fitted all too well into Claudia's stereotype. Murder ballads. There was the one that went:

> *Go away from my window*
> *You'll waken my father*
> *He's lying now, a-taking his rest,*
> *And in his hands he holds a weapon*
> *To kill the one that my heart loves best.*

He glanced across at Claudia. She stuck out her tongue at him and he laughed.

Then it was his turn. He picked up his guitar, sat on the stool, and sang her *Lord Bateman*. He'd chosen it very carefully.

He sang through the story, about how the proud Lord Bateman travels the world but is captured and imprisoned by the Sultan of Turkey. But then…

> *The Sultan had an only daughter,*
> *The fairest creature eyes did see…*
> *She stole the key to her father's prison*
> *And said 'Lord Bateman I will free.'*

Sophie, the Sultan's daughter, frees Lord Bateman, giving him food and drink and stealing him a ship. They farewell each other and both promise not to marry for seven years. That time done, the brave young woman follows him back to England, only to find Lord Bateman just in the process of being married. A traditional folk song would have ended there, with Sophie throwing herself off a tower in despair. Claudia had been right about that.

But in fact the song finishes with Lord Bateman sending his first bride packing and marrying Sophie instead.

> *Lord Bateman prepared another marriage,*
> *And both their hearts were full of glee.*
> *I will range no more to a foreign country*
> *Now since Sophie has a-crossed the sea.*

He stood up, took Claudia by the hand, and they left.

"Michael!" she said outside. "You have a wonderful voice. And you can actually *play* that damned thing."

"Well, yes," he said. That was the point.

"And I liked your song." She gazed up at him speculatively. "Come back to my room, and I'll play you some Philip Glass. The first Violin Concerto, maybe. You might like that."

"And if I don't?" Here was the crux of the matter.

"Well," she said. "I've got a great pair of headphones… I can listen to my stuff and you can listen to your stuff."

He strummed a happy chord on the guitar, and they walked on.

Handover

He started muttering again as Yvonne got out of the driver's seat and went around to his side of the car to help him out. Her heart sank.

"Please, Dad. You promised."

The old man glared at her as she brought around his walker and opened the door for him. He was unsteady on his feet — not surprising at the age of 90 — but once his hands were on the walker for balance, he could move surprisingly well. Now he headed off for the house at a steady, determined pace. "Dad!" she called after him in exasperation, as she was forced to take a few extra moments to retrieve her handbag and lock the car.

She strode after him towards the part-ruined house. The real-estate agent and the buyers would already be in there, she knew, having recognised the agent's car in the street.

After the fire, her father's inadequate insurance hadn't been enough to repair the house, just enough to do clean up what was left, just a little, and make it safe. But it was still a mess, with a smoke-blackened wall, a burnt-out staircase, and a hole in the living room ceiling through which you could see up to the next floor and then out to the blue sky. The upper floor had been almost completely burnt. But the stone outer wall of the house was still sound, and the building hadn't been condemned. Still, she'd been surpised when it sold, even considering the low price they had been forced to settle for.

That was when her father's muttering had started. And then the shouting. She tried to block her mind to the ugly, racist things he had said. It had taken a long while — days — to calm him down, to gain some grudging measure of acceptance.

"You have to sell," she had told him. "You can't live there any more, it's a wreck, and we can't afford to have it fixed up." *And you're not capable of looking after yourself any more*, she had thought, but of course not said. The fire had been his fault, some clothing left drying too close to an electric bar radiator, and her father falling asleep. He had been lucky to get out alive.

But while he had eventually acknowledged the truth of this, nothing seemed to reconcile him when he found out who was buying the property.

And now this. He had insisted on this meeting with the new owners, insisted stubbornly. *God, he can be stubborn*, Yvonne thought to herself. Sometimes she thought that stubbornness was her father's defining characteristic.

Her father did stop at the door of the house, though, so that she could catch up. Praying that he wouldn't burst out with another bigoted rant, she opened the door for him so they could enter what had been their old living room.

The agent was there with the new owners. Yvonne stifled a gasp when she saw one of them, immediately feeling ashamed by her reaction. But this young woman was… striking. Her skin was a deep, deep black, and she was astonishingly tall and thin. Not emaciated, just naturally very slim, dressed elegantly in a blue pant-suit which must have been custom-made for her. *My goodness*, Yvonne thought, *she's tall*. The dark young woman towered over the others.

The real-estate agent strode forward, professional charm uppermost, to shake her father's hand. "Mr Castles, so pleased to see you again!" Her father gave an ungracious grunt. The agent led him to one of the folding chairs which they had brought in, together with a card table for the documents.

"Let me introduce you to Nyanath and her family," the agent went on.

Nyanath, it appeared, was the tall young woman. The agent started to do the introductions, but stumbled a bit over the Sudanese names. Nyanath smoothly took over, introducing her father and mother, her teenage sister and two young brothers. Her English was excellent, though accented just a little. Yvonne recalled that the family had been here in Australia for some time now, though their application for refugee status had only just come through.

Yvonne's father remained stubbornly silent. *Well, maybe that's a blessing*, she thought. *If only he can keep his mouth shut through this whole thing, we'll all be better off.*

Yvonne made some polite conversation, asking about the family's plans. Nyanath, it seemed, was the bread-winner and so far the only one who spoke good English. She had a job in the city, and proposed to drive in and out every day. "But that's a good couple of hours each way!" Yvonne exclaimed.

"An hour and a half in good weather," Nyanath said. "Yes, that is fine. My father will be working here on the house, making it good. My brothers will help."

Yvonne's father cleared his throat, and her heart sank. *Oh God, here it comes*, she thought.

"I just want to say something," he said roughly.

Yvonne put her hand on his arm. "Dad..." she said warningly.

Stubbornly, he went on. "I just want to say... This was my house. I fixed it up, painted it, mended the roof. Brought my wife here. Raised our children in this house. Worked all my life in the cannery, but I always came home to this house. It's..." He started to tremble, and his voice failed him.

Nyanath knelt down beside him.

"I understand, sir. We will look after your house. We have been though some hard times, sir, and we have lost our own home, which we loved so dearly. We will make your house as new again, sir, and we will live here and be happy, just as you and your family were. For you, sir, it may seem an ending, but for us it is a new beginning."

There were tears in the old man's eyes now, but he looked up into her dark face and managed something like a smile.

He had trouble forming the words, but at last he said "Thank you. God bless you," he said. "And all your family."

The Poppies

It was a surprisingly long walk from the car park to the entrance, and Mark kept scampering on ahead, despite Sarah's best efforts to restrain him. Still, the path was safe enough, meandering past a lawn and under big oak trees until it reached the steps at the front of the Memorial. Mark ran up to the steps, and turned. He knew enough to stop there and wait for his mother to catch up with him.

She wasn't sure why her little son was so eager. She had tried to explain to him where they were going, and why, and he had seemed to understand, following her words with a sombre face. But he had only just turned four, and now that they were here, he seemed to think that it was just a great adventure.

Sarah stopped and held out her hand to him, which he took readily enough, not yet old enough to be embarrassed by holding his mother's hand. She turned away from the steps and looked down from the Memorial and along the long wide avenue, over the lake to Parliament House nearly four kilometres away.

There was something not quite right, she thought, about having your Parliament mounted on a hill, directly facing a distant memorial to war. It was as though the two buildings represented the extreme ends of a spectrum running from reasoned debate at one end to outright violence at the other. Or perhaps that was exactly the point that the planners were trying to make.

Mark tugged at her hand impatiently, interrupting her thoughts. She gave a small sigh. Often enough, that interruption to her mood had been a blessing, but here in this place, today, she found herself resenting it, just a little. "All right, then," she said. "Let's go in."

The steps were steep, but not too much for Mark's little legs, and soon they were at the glass doors and passing inside. To the left was a reception area. There were a number of tourists here, handing over back-packs and handbags to be stored in a cloakroom. Sarah waited patiently, keeping tight hold of Mark's hand. He was looking around, wide-eyed, at some of the exhibits, including a massive artillery piece, painted with camouflage colours. Sarah knew that if she let go of him, he would be up and climbing all over it.

Behind the counter a young woman barely out of her teens finished dealing with one of the tourists, and said briskly to Sarah: "Yes, can I help you?"

Now that she was here, Sarah found herself barely able to get out what she had to say. "Yes... I... that is..." She stoped, a bitter feeling growing in her. She felt herself desperate for some sympathy, and this young person didn't seem the right person to give it. "My husband... he was killed in Afghanistan two years ago..." She stopped again, unable to go on, tears welling in her eyes, making her feel angry with herself.

Fortunately, the young woman behind the counter seemed to sense Sarah's deep emotion. "Let me get one of the other staff members to help you, I haven't been here very long," she said.

She returned with a grey-haired man. "I'm so sorry to hear about your husband," he began. "Have you been here to the War Memorial before?"

Sarah shook her head, still unable to speak. The man looked down at Mark, now tugging insistently on Sarah's arm. "And is this your son? I don't suppose he remembers his father?"

She wiped away her tears and drew a breath. "No, not really. He was less than two when it happened."

"I'm Bob," said the man. "Here, young man, would you like this?" He held up a toy aeroplane.

"Oh yes!" said Mark eagerly, and then, with a sideways glance at his mother, "I mean yes, please."

"Good boy," said Bob, and handed over the plane. Mark immediately began swooping it around, making engine noises and, to Sarah's dismay, gun-firing sounds. She'd tried so hard to keep him away from war movies and toy weapons, any depiction of violence. Today, of course, was a huge exception, but it was unavoidable.

"And you are here today to…?" Bob asked.

"I understand that there are bronze plaques… the Roll of Honour?" Sarah said. "The council wrote to me last year when Richard's name was included for the first time. But… but I couldn't bring myself to come, then."

"Yes, the Roll is updated each Remembrance Day. It used to be that we only updated the panels at the end of each conflict. But, alas, some modern conflicts don't seem to have a clean ending, so now we do it annually. Would you like to see the panel with your husband's name?" Sarah nodded mutely.

"Perhaps you might like to place a poppy? Some unknown visitor first did that a few years ago, wedging a poppy into the gap between two panels, and it has rather caught on. We don't encourage it officially, of course, but now it seems an established tradition."

"Yes," she said, "yes, I would like that."

He brought her one, a bright red poppy flower made from a tough paper-based fabric. Mark, his attention caught by the colour, reached up for it, and Sarah handed it to him. "Be careful with it," she said, "use gentle hands." He nodded gravely, the toy plane momentarily forgotten in his other hand.

"If you would like to follow me, I'll show you where the panel is," Bob said. She nodded, and he led her outside into a bright courtyard with a reflecting pool. Arched passages on a higher level ran down the length of the courtyard. Bob pointed out to her the Eternal Flame burning at one end of the pool, then showed her the steps leading up to the second level.

She took the aeroplane from Mark so that she could hold his hand as they climbed up. As they reached the top, they came onto a balcony with a spectacular view down the avenue. In the distance, a huge Australian flag fluttered slowly atop the Parliament.

"Just here," said Bob gently, indicating a large bronze panel set into the stone wall at the end of the left-hand passage. Out of the corner of her eye, Sarah glimpsed scattered splotches of red, but her attention now was solely on the panel in front of her. She could see Richard's name, sharply outlined on the new panel, the bronze lettering still shiny.

"See," she said in a choked voice to her little son. "There's your Daddy's name, Mark." She bent down and lifted him up. He was heavy now, getting bigger every day. Awkwardly shifting his weight to one arm, she pointed out the name. "Can you push the flower in next to it?" she asked him.

He tried, but it was too hard. In the end, she put him down and pushed in the wire stem herself. There were many other poppies inserted between the panels, which showed the casualties of the 'modern' wars – Korea, Malaysia, Vietnam, Iraq and Afghanistan.

Sighing, with Mark fidgeting again, she turned way. To look for the first time along the arcaded passage. It was lined with bronze panels, too, stretching the full length of the building. It was carpeted with red poppies, hundreds and hundreds of them.

She stared at them for a long while, silent, and then she looked across the courtyard at the other passage. It was identical — dozens of bronze panels running along the wall, and every one crammed with poppies placed there by loving and grieving close family members or their descendants. Hundreds and hundreds of poppies, maybe thousands.

"How many?" she asked at last.

"Deaths?" Bob replied. He shook his head slowly. "More than a hundred thousand. Not a lot, perhaps, compared to some countries, but then Australia has never had a large population." He shrugged sadly. "Relative to our population, a hundred thousand deaths in war is indeed a great many. The First World War was the worst for us, in that regard."

"Not a lot?" she asked, disbelieving. "Think of their wives, their mothers, their children..." She looked down then at Mark, now happily playing with his aeroplane again, making zooming and bang, bang noises. Was there no end to this?

She thought back to her life with Richard, to the three short years she'd had with him before he was killed. She had tried, tried so hard, to be the good military wife. But every night that he'd been overseas she had lain awake, dreading what would happen to him. And then it had happened, in the worst possible way, in an unexpected way. One of the Afghan soldiers Richard had been training had turned his rifle on Richard and shot him dead, right there inside the supposedly safe military base. But there was no safety any more, no more certainties.

Why had she come here today? Out of a sense of duty, she supposed. There had been the military funeral, of course, the sympathy from the politicians, the heartfelt eulogies from his teammates. But she had hardly been able to feel anything through her numbness, and had shed few tears.

This bronze panel was such a small thing in comparison, a single name on a piece of metal. But it joined a hundred thousand others. Maybe that was the point.

Mark was running up and down the passage, his little body moving in and out of the patches of sunlight and shade, flying his toy aeroplane.

Not him, she thought fiercely. I don't care what I have to do. No matter what it takes. I will not let it happen to him.

He ran up to her and looked up eagerly into her face. "Mummy?"

"Yes, Mark?"

"When I grow up, I want to shoot all the bad guys, just like my Daddy."

Note of Triumph

In threadbare clothing with many patches, some barefoot, some short, some tall, all of them skinny; girls with plaited hair and shy smiles, boys with grubby faces and wide grins. Here they all came.

The children always came running when the Salvation Army band arrived in the street.

Mary Bennett smiled to see the children, but it was their parents who they were really trying to reach. Here some of them came: mothers wiping their hands on their aprons, or carrying babies, or holding hands with toddlers who were towing them along toward the band. And some of the men, too, glowering from the doorways of the terraced houses, or lounging outside, smoking hand-rolled cigarettes, their faces shaded by the flat wide-brimmed caps that they wore. She knew that those men were only there because now they had no jobs to go to.

The band drew up in the middle of the long cobbled street and prepared to play.

All the old favourite hymns, of course. That's what people wanted to hear. Well, the adults did. The children just loved the spectacle of the band: the Salvation Army uniforms, the brass instruments, the cymbals. There wasn't much entertainment in their lives outside of this. They were too poor even to pay for tickets to the Christmas pantomimes in the town hall at a halfpenny a head. Mary smiled at the face of one little red-haired boy staring up at her, eyes wide with anticipation.

Mary lifted her beloved cornet and joined in as the music began. A little flame of joy began in her, and she wondered, just for an instant, if it wasn't sinful to enjoy playing so much. She was still quite young, in her late twenties. There had to be some joy in life, didn't there? And it was all for the glory of God. Surely it was no more wrong than admiring the beauty of a stained glass window?

In the intervals between the music, their leader Robert gave a short homily and the band handed out leaflets and extracts from the Bible.

It was after one such interval that Mary realised with a terrible shock that her cornet was gone. She had put it down on the cobbles, standing on its flared mouth, just between her feet. But when she reached down for it, it had vanished. She looked wildly around. Down a little alley, she glimpsed the back of a running child. A child with red hair.

"It was little Billy Keenan, I saw him!", piped up a little girl. "He nicked your trumpet, miss."

"No it weren't," called out a grubby little boy. "It were that Jackie from down the canal."

"Yer both wrong," said a tall boy with crooked teeth. "Freddy Rowland done it, him what lives near the mill."

Mary looked despairingly at the children who had spoken, at their grins and their sly looks at each other and knew that they were all three of them lying to her. Her heart sank, not only for her own loss, but also for the recognition of how quickly sin descended onto these poor children.

Robert was already playing the next hymn, and looked across in puzzlement when Mary failed to join in. She indicated her empty hands, with tears in her eyes. The children who had spoken to her before had now vanished into the crowd.

The band leader was sympathetic. Tall, his hair nearly all white now, his face was grave as she explained what had happened during the next interval.

"Don't worry, Mary. I'm sure we can find you another cornet from our store. Or we can requisition you another from headquarters."

"But that's not the point," she said sorrowfully. "It was my father's instrument, don't you remember? He taught me how to play when I was quite young, and gave me his cornet when he was too ill to play himself."

"Ah, yes." He looked thoughtfully around. "Perhaps, then, you might spend some time looking in the pawn shops around here. Surely that's where the young miscreant will take it in the hope of a sixpence or two."

She nodded and tried to smile, but without much real hope.

On the way back to her rented room that night she did pass by several of the pawn shops that littered the main street of the town. But although some of them did have musical instruments – three battered old accordions, several mouth-organs, and even one trombone with a twisted slide – none of them had her stolen cornet among their goods. Perhaps it was too soon to expect that? The thief might just be waiting for an opportunity to visit the pawnbrokers.

Mary sat alone in her room that night, shivering a little. Winter was coming on and she would have to pay her landlady for some coal soon. She looked sadly at the place on the dresser where she had always kept the cornet. She never practiced here, of course, she would have been evicted for creating a disturbance. But still, she missed it, and allowed herself another few tears. *How silly, how sinful, to grieve for a mere piece of metal*, she thought, and managed to bring her tears under control.

Her prayers that night were not for herself, but for the young thief, that he might be guided away from the paths of sin.

Some weeks passed. Mary visited the pawn shops again, but to no avail. She was given a battered old cornet from the local Army store and a requisition was made for a replacement. But this, she knew, could take months. There was always a backlog of orders at the factory.

The national economy went from bad to worse. More and more men were out of work. Families were being evicted, and many more were having trouble feeding their children. The Salvation Army began operating mobile soup kitchens, small vans moved from place to place by horses. Mary agreed to help out with these. Her life was otherwise empty.

It was on one of these missions that she saw the red-headed boy again, waiting in the queue for soup with other children. He reached the head of the line and lifted up his broken-handled cup. Mary reached out, grasped his wrist firmly and said in a voice like that of an avenging angel: "*You are a thief!*"

She hadn't meant to be so loud, so harsh, it had happened on an impulse. She was normally so kind and quiet, now she had shocked herself.

The boy squirmed in her grip, trying to pull away. "No miss, no! I didn't nick your trumpet!"

"Then how do you know that was what was stolen?" she asked, her face still grim.

He squirmed again, and the little van rocked a little with his struggle to get away. Robert, who had been doling out soup on the other side of the van, came over and stared at the confrontation.

"Young man," he said, "we passed a policeman just around the last corner. Shall I go and fetch him?"

The boy looked around wildly, his eyes rolling. "No, no!"

"Then tell this lady what you did with her cornet. Did you sell it? Where?"

The boy stopped pulling back and almost sank to his knees. Mary now found that she was holding him up. "No," he whispered. "I din' sell it. I still got it. Please…"

Robert looked at Mary. "I can manage here by myself for a while. Why don't you go with this boy so he can return it to you? Mind now," he said sternly to the boy, "if you give this lady back what you stole then we will say no more about it. But if you give her any trouble, then I shall fetch the policeman. Do you understand?"

The red-haired boy nodded glumly, and stood up straight again. Mary released his arm and climbed down from the back of the van.

She half-expected him to have run off again, but he stood waiting for her. "This way," he mumbled, and started off down the street.

"What's your name?" Mary asked, as kindly as she could.

"Tommy. Tommy Sanders," he said. "It's just down here. My Mam... she won't half belt me when she finds out."

"Have you stolen other things, Tommy?"

He shook his head vigorously. "No, nothin'. Your trumpet was the first thing I ever stole, honest to God."

"You mustn't take the Lord's name in vain, Tommy. And what you stole isn't really a trumpet. It's called a cornet. Why did you take it?"

He looked up at her in wonder. "It... it was so beautiful. And you played it real nice, Miss."

Mary managed a smile at that, even though it wasn't much of an answer.

In front of one of the houses in the terrace, a weary-looking woman, her hair tied back in a blue scarf, was on her knees, whitening the front step of her house with a block of white stone. A silly custom, Mary thought, but one which she knew no proud housewife in this area of the country would even consider omitting.

The woman looked up. "Tommy Sanders, are you in trouble again? Am I going to fetch the strap?"

"No Mam, no!"

"It's all right, Mrs Sanders," Mary said. For some reason she didn't want to see young Tommy punished. "Tommy found something that I lost, that's all, and he is going to give it back to me."

Tommy's mother looked at him sharply, her eyes narrowed. "Tommy…" she began warningly.

"Can I get in, Mam? I'll jump over the step, honest."

She nodded, and he leapt over the step and ran into the house. Mary wondered what she could say to his mother; she wasn't good at small talk with strangers. But Mrs Sanders turned back to scrubbing the step, and Tommy returned in a few minutes, carrying a bundle wrapped up in an old towel. He leapt over the step again, and looked up at Mary.

By an unspoken mutual agreement, they walked a little way down the street, out of the sight and hearshot of Tommy's Mam.

Tommy unwrapped the bundle and rather reluctantly handed the cornet to Mary. She gave a little gasp. The old instrument had never looked so good. Its steel shone like silver. Every inch of it had been polished. She looked at Tommy.

"You've taken great care of it," she said. "Tell me, Tommy, have you tried playing it?"

Tommy looked down and shuffled his feet. "Sometimes, when me Mam and Dad are out."

"And what happened? Show me." She found herself handing back the gleaming cornet.

He looked up at her with a little frown. "I can't play a tune on it, like," he said. "But I practiced as much as I could, and now I can make a good sound." He lifted it to his lips and blew a perfect note. That was half the battle, with a brass instrument.

Mary stood looking at him, considering. "Would you like to learn to play?" she said at last.

There was a sudden flash of eagerness in his young face, but it swiftly vanished into gloom. "Me Mam can't pay for lessons. And now I don't have the trumpet any more."

"I told you, it's called a cornet. What if I taught you, Tommy?"

The eagerness was back, but he was almost speechless. "I… I…"

"I'll tell you what, Tommy," she said, barely believing what she was saying. "If you learn to play, learn to play really well, and come along to play with the band, I'll let you keep the cornet."

He looked down in wonderment at the cornet, then lifted it to his lips and sounded one long, loud, clear note of triumph.

The Project

When Karen dropped Emma off outside my place that Saturday, I thought I saw a half-smile on her face. That was puzzling.

"Your Mum seems more cheerful this time," I said to Emma. The last time she had left Emma with me, a month ago, Karen had given me her usual death-ray glare.

"Oh, that's because she's got a boyfriend now," said Emma blithely. A stab to the heart. *Damn*, I thought for a second. And then, a moment later I rallied and managed: "Well, that's good then. I guess. What's he like?"

My 12-year-old daughter shrugged. "OK. He's just a suit, though, from where she works. Pretty boring."

"Well, then. Good for her," I managed unconvincingly. I still wasn't really over the divorce and its bitter aftermath in the Family Court, but I was getting there. Slowly.

"Do you want to get some lunch?" I asked Emma. "McDonalds again?"

The response was surprising. "No, yuk! Tastes awful. I'm *so* over junk food."

"You are?"

"Yep. I've been watching *Master Chef*, it's great. I might go into catering when I finish school."

Emma had just started high school. Her intended careers so far had included airline pilot, lawyer and — of all things — speech pathologist. Now it was catering. We would see.

"Well, then...?"

"How about we go up to your flat and you make me some lunch?"

"Me? You're the one watching *Master Chef.*"

"Nope, I'm your guest, aren't I? Besides, I want to see what you eat these days."

What I ate was mostly take-away pizza and microwaved noodles, but I wasn't going to tell Emma that. Picking up her pink suitcase, I led the way up the stairs and into my cheap two-bedroom flat. Emma would be staying for the weekend, and I had made up a trundle bed for her in the second bedroom, which normally doubled as my study.

I had done my best to clean up, but Emma looked around critically.

"You need to dust occasionally, Dad," she said as I dumped the surprisingly heavy suitcase on the bed. Then she marched me off into the kitchen and opened the fridge. There wasn't a lot in there, except for a six-pack of beer short one bottle.

She peered in, making tsk-ing sounds. "Hmmm, you've got a few eggs, I won't ask how old they are." She opened the freezer compartment. "Oh yuk, Dad! Did you know there's a frozen bottle of beer in here? It's all burst and broken."

I was feeling chastised and foolish. "Er, I must have put it in there to cool down one day and forgot about it."

"Well, *I'm* not going to touch it. You can get it out of there later on. Wearing a pair of gloves. OK, then, at least there are eggs. You can make me scrambled eggs. I've got to chat to Becky." And she promptly sat down on my couch, pulled out her phone and started messaging at a rate of knots. I was surprised that she had lasted that long.

Ten minutes later she had exchanged missives with at least a dozen friends, and I had a burnt yellow-black mess in a frying pan.

Emma looked at it in disgust. "Geez, Dad!"

"Well, I don't do much cooking."

"I can tell. OK, come on, where are the nearest shops?"

"Just around the corner. There's a good pizza place..."

She glared at me, a glare not yet as highly-sharpened as her mother's, but well on the way. "We're going *shopping*," she declared.

An hour later we were back, with a bag stuffed full. Fresh eggs, milk, bread, vegetables and herbs.

"By the way," she said casually as we came up the stairs, "I'm twisting Mum's arm to let me stay with you every second week instead of once a month. I think she's gonna give in. I can be *very* persuasive. Unless..." she said, looking up at me with a moment's vulnerable apprehension, "unless you don't want that?"

I shook my head in wonder. "No, that would be great."

Inside the flat, Emma made scrambled eggs on toast, forcing me to follow every step. "You shouldn't turn the heat up too high. That's mostly what you did wrong last time. And, oh, never put milk into the eggs. Just a dash of water. OK?"

We sat and ate in companionable silence for a while. Then she asked: "Are you seeing anyone yet?"

I spluttered out some eggs. "No. And it's none of your business."

"Yes it is," she said simply. "You need to move on, Dad."

I stood up in irritation. "You've been watching too much TV. Besides, I could ask you the same question." Emma was attending a public co-Ed school. Our plans of sending her to an exclusive girls-only school had vanished with the split-up and the cost of the divorce.

Emma coloured only very slightly. "No, but there's this boy in the next year I have my eye on. I'll give him a couple of years and we'll see how he turns out. We weren't talking about me, though. You're dodging the question."

"Well…" I said reluctantly. It seemed so *wrong* talking to my daughter about this. "I don't get to meet many women outside of the office. And in the office, well, it gets awkward. If it doesn't work out, that is."

Emma narrowed her eyes at me. "Well, we'll work on that later." What did *that* mean?

But she was going on: "You'll need to make this flat look a bit more enticing, though. Clean it up more often, for a start. And I've got a present for you." She zipped off into the room where I'd left her suitcase.

She brought back a large framed photo which must just have squeezed into the case.

It was a picture of Emma herself, taken a year or so ago, sitting at a table with a floppy hat pulled over her eyes and a straw sticking out of her mouth, looking highly casual. It had been our last family holiday together, and we'd stayed at a farm. It was a great shot, and one I had forgotten about.

"This can be the first thing you put up on your walls," she said. They were indeed almost entirely bare. "Did I tell you about the project I have to do for school?" she asked in a dizzying segue.

"No," I said weakly, with tears in my eyes from looking at the photo.

"It's called the Community Service Project. We have to find someone in the community who needs help, and do something for them. Becky has taken on this girl from Somalia who needs English lessons, and Jade has picked this old lad who is going blind, and is reading books to her. And for my project..."

I could see where this was going.

"...I've picked you."

Storm Front

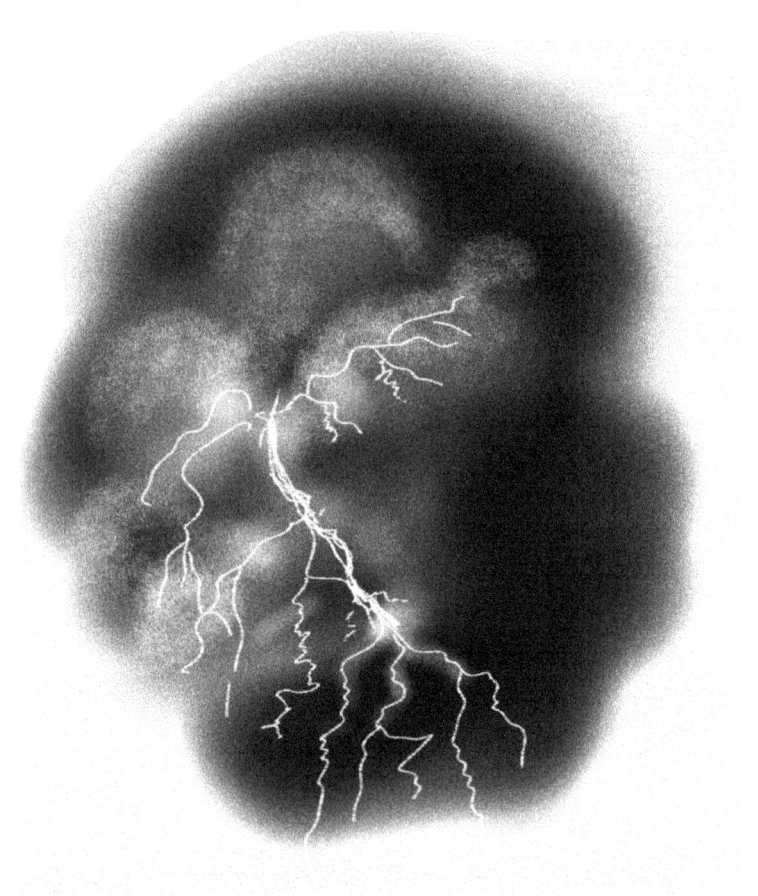

Lightning flashed. Long moments later, the accompanying thunder rolled in, shaking the house and frightening old Shep, who scuttled under the couch, and stayed there, whining.

Bob went to the doorway, and stood looking out.

"Will it rain?" Mary asked anxiously, coming to join Bob as they looked out over their parched property in the late afternoon. "Please God, let it rain."

There were dark clouds on the horizon, but that meant nothing. There had been the promise of rain many times before, all coming to nothing.

It had been four years now, with hardly a drop. Their crops had failed every year. Now they were deeply in debt to the bank. If the drought continued for another year, they would lose the farm.

"What's God got to do with it?" asked Bob, bitterly. "How many times now have we prayed for rain, and nothing came of it?"

"It's not for us to question the ways of God," Mary said sincerely. "He must have a plan for us."

"A plan? I'll tell you what his plan is. He hates all of us, wants to make us suffer. He's good at that, too damned good."

"You mustn't say that..."

"I'll say what I damned well please!" Bob shouted, and struck at her with the back of his hand. Mary stumbled and fell, crying out. Shep poked his head out from under the couch and growled, baring his fangs.

"Hell!" said Bob, bending down to her as she sobbed. "I'm so sorry, love." Suddenly, he too began to cry, gently at first, and then great racking sobs. Mary reached up and stroked his head.

Bob and Mary sat hugging on the floor, looking out together.

Outside, it began to rain, softly at first, and then at last building into a torrential downpour.

Trick or Treat

In retrospect, Mary-Jean Broadbent realised that the trouble must have started at number 10.

It was so hard, and rather dispiriting, to try to organize a proper trick-or-treat here in Australia. Australians didn't seem to quite *get* Halloween, although some kids did try to participate in a half-hearted way. Too many households here just weren't prepared for the kids' arrival and didn't have any treats ready. And you just *couldn't* get the right kind of pumpkins here to make proper jack-o-lanterns.

Mary-Jean didn't usually miss America so much. She liked living in Australia, she really did, but times like Halloween and Thanksgiving were the most difficult to bear and made her feel very homesick.

Her three boys were so very enthusiastic to go out trick-or-treating, though. They were all dressed as ninjas, they looked just the cutest things. There was a big revival here of the old Samurai TV series, a remake by the Japanese, and ninjas and samurai were the big thing now. So nothing would do for the boys but that they go dressed as ninjas. They did look great, she thought admiringly as she left home with them. She wasn't prepared to let them go walking around the neighbourhood by themselves, not when she still didn't really know the neighbours all that well.

Tagging along with the boys was little Jemima from next door, dressed in pink with wings, a glittery crown and a silver wand.

Their first stop was Mrs Stavropolous at number 8. A nice old lady, living by herself now that her husband had died, just a few months ago. She didn't quite understand the trick-or-treat thing, nor did she understand what the boys were dressed as, though she understood Jemima's fairy costume well enough. After a long search, hunting through drawers, she found some candy and handed it out gravely to the four children.

"Thanks so much," said Mary-Jean, and went on to number 10. Afterwards, she thought to herself that she should have been less naive, but then, how was she to know?

The couple living at number 10 were in their late fifties, but didn't behave much like people of their age. Mary-Jean had heard that during the 1960s – or whenever that counter-culture thing had been – they had both been hippies. Fair enough for those times, she supposed, but neither of them seemed to have realised that time had moved on.

The door was opened by Galadriel – surely that couldn't be her real name? A buxom woman, dressed in a loose Indian floral-print dress, and wearing a bead necklace. She was delighted to see Mary-Jean and the kids, and welcomed them into her cramped kitchen.

"Oh, so cute! What are you dressed as, dears? Ninjas? And a fairy! How lovely. How wonderful that you should come today!" Galadriel exclaimed. "I've been cooking! Here you go, children. These are called Carob Delights. Yummy!" And, in an aside to Mary-Jean: "No sugar, you know, dear, it's so bad for young children."

The children, eyeing and tasting the brown lumps, looked as though 'yummy' was the last word in the English language they would have applied to these objects.

"Now," said Galadriel to Mary-Jean, "you must have a spot of sherry. I'm very partial to it myself. Let's just have one while the children are enjoying their treats."

Mary-Jean felt it impolite to refuse, so she gulped down the sweet sherry and then she made their excuses and went on.

There was no-one at home at number 12. At number 14 lived a young couple with two children of their own, a boy and a girl, who came to the door with their mother. "Trick or treat?" the mother repeated. "Well, what if I ask for the trick?" Mary-Jean's sons had obligingly spun rubber throwing-stars at the lady, who laughed and handed over prepared bags of candy. Now this was more like it.

It was as they approached number 16 that Mary-Jean started to feel a little odd.

For a while, just for a little while, she could swear that she saw little Jemima flap her fairy wings and lift up from the sidewalk.

No one home at number 16, but she had to keep calling the boys back into order. They kept doing extraordinary things like leaping backwards up onto the roof of a house, or into a tree. Jemima was definitely floating up higher and higher, and Mary-Jean had to grab hold of her hand to make sure she didn't just plain float away.

Mr Tanaka lived at number 18, but Mary-Jean didn't think he would understand the Halloween tradition at all. Or would he? Did the Japanese celebrate Halloween? Perhaps they did. She didn't seem to be able to remember. They did play baseball, she knew that, so maybe it would be all right.

They knocked and almost immediately the door opened. Mr Tanaka stood there, impossibly tall and filling the doorway. Dressed in full Samurai uniform, helmet, grim leather mask and all. He came out, swinging his katana swords and the boys started casting their throwing stars, which hit with solid metal thunks, knocking off sparks. They all whipped out long knives she was sure they hadn't had before, and slashed at Mr Tanaka. Even Jemima, somehow taller now, was casting huge fireballs from her wand, which burst against Mr Tanaka's chest.

Despite these attacks, Mr Tanaka thundered out and rushed towards Mary-Jean, his twin swords flashing in the street-light. He swung… and cut Mary-Jean's head right off. She gave a gasp and stumbled back. Somehow she remained conscious. She looked down and could see her head just sitting there on the ground, looking startled and rather offended.

Then everything went dark for a time.

"Mrs Broadbent, are you all right, ma'am?" Little Mr Tanaka, dressed in a perfectly ordinary sweater and dark pants, was bending over her as she sat with her back to a tree in his front yard.

"Mom, mom, are you OK?" asked the boys in concert. Jemima was crying and demanding to be taken home.

Though she still felt a little woozy, Mary-Jean was indeed recovering. "Just a dizzy spell," she said. "Something I drank, I think."

Next year, she thought, *we won't do Halloween.*

In Concert

They were running late, but barring any traffic hold-ups they should still make it in time, Emma thought. It had been a struggle to dress herself, do her make-up and then get the two girls into their performance dresses and their hair done. All without any help from Jim, she thought bitterly.

She strapped the girls into the back seat of the car. They were being uncooperative and squirmed around as they chattered together in excitement. As Emma finally slipped into the driver's seat she pulled out her phone and sent off a quick text:

wr R u?

Without waiting for a reply she started off and headed for the Concert Hall. Charlotte and Sienna were going to an expensive girls-only primary school in the eastern suburbs, and their annual school concert was a major production, frequently including elaborate props and an original score. One year their Christmas production had featured actual live camels to transport the three Wise Men. It explained where some of the exorbitant fees went, she supposed.

Just before she reached the car park outside the hall, her phone binged, but she ignored it until she had pulled safely into a parking spot. Ever since one of her friends had been killed by a texting driver,

Emma was careful never to use her phone when she drove, particularly when she had the girls in the car.

She pulled the phone out of her handbag and glanced at it. The message was from Jim, of course:

sorry honey big client confab running late i'll meet you inside

Emma swore under her breath. At least Jim had his own ticket with him. From long experience, she'd been insistent that he take it. Was he really still at the office? Was it another woman? On balance, she thought he was telling the truth. Jim loved Charlotte and Sienna as much as she did, wouldn't deliberately stay away from the concert. If only this kind of thing didn't happen so often.

She shepherded the girls to the stage door, and handed them over gratefully to their music teacher and then found her way to her seat.

Half an hour later the house lights went down and the lights lit up the stage for the opening number. Beside Emma, Jim's empty seat felt like an open wound.

The performance ran on and finally it was her daughters' turn to shine. As they came forward together into the spotlight, lovely in their white and red dresses, Emma felt like screaming. What would happen, she thought, if I just stood up and started screaming out loud? But no, she couldn't spoil the girls' big moment.

They sang beautifully together. Beautifully. And Emma really did enjoy it, but not without a constant dragging despair that Jim wasn't here to watch them. When the sisters had finished, there was a storm of applause from the audience. And right in the middle of it, she felt her phone vibrate. A message from Jim.

on my way now be there soon

That's when she did scream, or at least let out a little furious howl of frustration. Fortunately, the applause drowned it out.

Jim dropped into the seat beside her just as the grand finale number was under way. He began muttering an apology, but she punched him, hard, on the shoulder. It must have hurt. He flinched, and his lips set into a firm line.

Outside, as they waited for the girls to come out, their privacy partially ensured by the hubbub of the audience, she let him have it, a long white-hot diatribe about his inability to be there when his family needed him, how inconsiderate he was, how much more important his career seemed to be to him than his family. Jim took it all without responding or trying to defend himself, his face just setting into a grimmer and grimmer expression.

They drove home, in separate cars of course, Emma with the children in the back, over-excited now and becoming fractious with each other.

Once inside, she and Jim barely spoke to one another while they managed to get the girls undressed and in to their beds. At last it was done, and they returned to the lounge room.

"Jim…" she began.

"Honey, don't start out on me again. I couldn't get away from that damned meeting. We're going to court with the Amundsen case next week."

"But it's *all the time*, there's always something, some meeting or other or you have to work late on a contract. It's all the time."

"I..." Suddenly, shockingly, Jim began to cry. It began with a sudden gasp and then he put his face in his hands, sat down abruptly, and sobbed. Emma was at first astonished, and then, quickly, like the sun coming out from behind a cloud, her mood changed from anger to solicitude. She knelt down and hugged him until his sobs stopped. She felt at sea, lost. He had never, ever, broken down like this before.

"Do you think..." he forced out. Paused, regaining his breath. "Do you think I *like* having missed the girls singing in the concert? Do you think I *want* to live this way? I feel like I'm a rat on a treadmill, and I can't get off." He paused a long minute, angrily wiping the tears from his face. "Old Carnegie collared me on the way out of the meeting, that's why I was so late. They want me to go to Sydney to sort out some case they are running there. Want me to stay for up to six weeks, starting on the first of next month."

Just stating it, not with any angry tone, yet with her heart sinking she said: "But... you'll miss Sienna's birthday. And our anniversary."

"I told him I would think about it. He didn't want to hear that, but I said I would have to talk to you. He was pretty snarky when I said that."

Emma was still hugging him. "Will it affect your prospects for becoming an associate?"

"If I just say no? Absolutely. But look, I've been thinking. Been thinking for quite a while, really." He straightened up, gently shrugged off her arm. "Emma, how much do you like this house? The school the girls go to? Your friends around here?"

She was silent for a long, long time. It was her turn to think hard. After an endless time, during which she became conscious of the clock ticking softly on the wall, she said: "Not as much as I love you and the kids."

He looked hard at her. "You know my Dad's been wanting to retire, give up his practice? I've been thinking… maybe I should offer to take it over."

Jim's father had a small suburban solicitor's firm out in the western suburbs. Handling wills and helping small businesses with their legal affairs. Compared to the big city legal firm where Jim worked now, it was like comparing an ant to an elephant.

Emma's head was whirling. She started thinking about her friends, who were mostly the mothers of other girls at her daughters' school. About the constant pressure to keep up with them, to look as good or better than they did, about their constant one-upping over their latest gadgets. Emma and Jim had been intending to put in an expensive home theatre in their house, really only because their friends mostly had them. Were they friends... or just competitors?

Jim was going on, eager now. "It would slash our income, by a heap. But we could sell this house. It's not a great seller's market right now, but even so we have enough equity that we would at least have a good deposit for a house over in the west. Swap our cars for cheaper ones. I think we could manage. I know that the girls would hate having to leave their fancy school and start at a public school over there, but they're good kids, I think they would adjust. It would be tough for a while, for all of us. But I would be home every night. And I would be less likely to drop dead from a heart attack in my forties."

Emma knelt there, her hands on her knees, staring at the carpet. Was she really ready to give up this lifestyle? She thought it all through. Thought about how she had felt sitting there tonight waiting for Jim to arrive at the concert. Thought about how unhappy she had been over the last few years, despite the nice house, despite the car, despite the clothes, the shoes and the jewellery. Just stuff, she thought at last. Just more and more stuff.

She looked up at him at last.

"OK," she said. "Let's do it."

On the Edge

Ricky got up before dawn. His father would have called it a miracle, he thought bitterly.

Leaving his bed unmade, he left the rustic cabin he was sharing with his cousin and went out into the frosty air.

The body heat of the three horses in the stable took off the chill in there, but his fingers were still cold and clumsy as he did his best to saddle up the grey the way he had been shown. Under his breath, he kept up a constant stream of cursing, swearing at each fumbled buckle, each twisted strap. But finally it was done, and he climbed up and urged the mare out of the stable.

It was becoming lighter now, but there was still a heavy mist shrouding the trees as he inexpertly managed the horse along the bridle path. Birds were starting to call tentatively, but he barely heard them, could hardly think of anything outside of himself. He was consumed with savage thoughts of how he had been treated, of the futility of it all, and by the constant feelings of guilt and humiliation dragging on his mind.

The mare was reluctant under his clumsy riding. She was probably as cold as he was, he thought belatedly. She kept folding back her ears and slowing down until he kicked with his heels to make her go on.

It became a little easier after a while as the sun started to come up and the woodland brightened. He turned the horse's head to the right at the fork in the path, and they started to climb up towards the bluff. It was slow work, but the path was not steep, and the horse seemed to be warming up and was becoming resigned to the way he was riding her.

Eventually they were above the tops of the trees, and then above the mist. Ricky stopped for a moment, jolted out of his misery by the stunning view. A blanket of soft sun-lit cloud lay over the forest, with only a few tree-tops poking out here and there.

But the respite was only for a second. He pushed the horse on, until they reached the level clearing behind the big flat rock that jutted from the top of the bluff, overlooking the forest below.

He climbed off the horse, almost falling off, and looped the reins around a tree branch.

Stumbling a little, he started to walk towards the rock. Every footstep seemed a struggle, as though his feet were stuck in mud, though there was nothing to impede him on the dry earth. He forced himself onwards. He was almost to the edge when the mare gave a snort of derision and he looked back, alarmed, as she gave a shake of her head, pulled the reins loose, and trotted off.

"Shit!" If the horse was lost, his uncle would be totally pissed. He hesitated a long moment, feeling a tiny inner sense of relief that he would barely acknowledge, and then tried to follow the horse. He should at least tie her up properly, he could leave that well done at least. But teasingly, she moved away as he approached, kept moving away from him, always out of reach. "Damn, damn, damn, damn, damn!" he kept on saying, beginning to sob with frustration.

That's when his uncle rode up on the brown stallion.

He gave Ricky a wry look and cantered after the mare, which didn't seem reluctant to be caught. His uncle brought the two horses back to where Ricky was standing, feeling stupid. As usual.

"Come up for the view, did you?" asked his uncle lightly, as he tied the horses securely to a tree. "Come on, then." And he led the way to the flat rock and to the cliff edge.

They stood for a moment, looking out over the trees and the snow-covered tops of the higher hills beyond his uncle's property.

"It's not high enough here, you know," said his uncle conversationally.

"What?" Ricky was startled.

"Not high enough to kill you outright. You'd just end up with some badly broken bones. Pretty damn painful. Take you a long while to die."

Ricky's mouth dropped open. "How did you know…?"

"I'm not stupid, that's how." His lined, suntanned face looked down at Ricky. "Not as stupid as your father, anyhow. Want to talk about it?"

Ricky sank down and put his face in his hands. After a long, long time, he managed a nod. He opened his mouth, but nothing came out.

His uncle sat down beside him. Their legs dangled over the cliff edge.

"Maybe I can make it easier, then," his uncle said. "I knew when my sister married your father that there would eventually be something like this. Listen, Ricky, it's not a sin, no matter what your Dad says."

Shocked, Ricky looked at his uncle, and then away across the landscape. "Everything seems to be a sin," he choked out. "At least, he says so."

His uncle gave a quiet grunt. "I was a bit surprised that he let you come and stay with us."

"It was Mum, she made him. There was a big row."

His uncle sighed. "I don't suppose your Dad thinks that I'm much of a Christian, at least not by his lights. But I reckon I'm as good a Christian as he is, anyhow. And I don't believe that God would create our bodies the way he has, given us the drives that we have, filled fourteen-year-old boys full of raging hormones, just to be able to then put up a big stop sign and tell any poor kid who crosses the line that they are going to Hell."

Ricky sat there feeling astonished. No adult had ever talked to him like this before.

"What was it?" his uncle asked. "What triggered off the row?"

Ricky shuffled uncomfortably. "Well, he won't let me use the computer unless he's with me to see what I'm doing. So I..." He stopped.

"Go on."

Ricky blushed. "He... he found some... some magazines I'd hidden." To his own astonishment, he found himself giving a laugh. "Not very well."

His uncle laughed out loud. "I had magazines like that at your age. And I'll give any odds that your father did, too."

Ricky gaped. "You mean..."

"Can't prove it, of course, but I would be very surprised if he didn't. Look, Ricky, your father has his own views, and you have to live with him, at least for the next few years. But you don't have to accept everything he says. Make up your own mind about things. Come and stay with us whenever you like, whenever it gets too much." His uncle smiled. "Oh, and hide your magazines better next time."

They gazed over the forest together. It was starting to warm up.

"Come on," said his uncle. "Your aunt will have the hide off me if we're late for breakfast."

Swear not by the Moon

The full moon had been rising, silver and serene, when they first made love.

Eager for each other, desperate, they had left a trail of scattered clothes and then coupled in the moonlight as it streamed in through the uncurtained window of his apartment.

That was the first time. There were many times after that, both day and night. But because of the special joy of that first climax they delighted to repeat it when the moon was full.

"Think of me as your own personal werewolf", he'd said, and she had laughed.

Her regrets came later.

She should, she thought, have known better. He was her boss, after all.

He was, of course, eager to conceal their relationship from the rest of the office. Too many complications if everyone knows, that's what he had said. So during their working day, they were cool to each other, keeping their feelings under control. For her, at least, it was difficult, and she carefully watched what she said to him, how she looked at him when there were others present.

But it seemed that as even as her passion waxed strong, his had been waning.

On a moonless night they walked through the gardens near his apartment. The sky was full of stars and she was marvelling at their beauty when for her their glory suddenly and forever vanished.

He told her there was someone else.

She raged at him, of course, wept, hammered at him with her fists. But to no avail. He was cold, contemptuous, turned and walked away from her without another word.

She stayed away from the office on the next day, and the next, sobbing in her bedroom most of the time. On the third day she forced herself to dry her tears and go back to work.

He avoided her as much as he could, and she him. But there were times when they had to be in the same room together: staff meetings, documents she had to discuss with him. The dark circles under her eyes grew and were barely covered in make-up. Her work began to suffer.

While the firm's policies wouldn't allow him to fire her outright, he could certainly recommend it to the partners, and before she knew it she was out on the street and looking for another job.

That's when she discovered that she was pregnant.

She confronted him, literally grabbing him by the elbow as he came out of the office block where she had once worked. He denied that the child was his, claimed it was someone else's seed, laughed scornfully when she demanded a paternity test. But it couldn't have been anyone else. There was no one else. Since their first time, there had been no one else for her.

She had been thinking about an abortion, agonising over the decision, when nature stepped in and did the job for her.

The miscarriage changed something in her, made her stronger somehow. She formed a resolve, made a plan. She had nothing to lose, she thought, her life was over.

Perhaps if she had been reading the newspapers or watching the television news she might have been aware of what was expected that night, but these things were of no interest to her now.

As it was, there was again a perfect harmony between earth and sky that night. The night when she waited for him, late in the evening, outside his apartment block. With the long, sharp knife concealed up her sleeve.

As she spied him walking towards her, the moon began to turn a bloody red.

The Despised

Brian had been on a peaceful afternoon walk through the parklands that Sunday when it happened.

Something behind him struck a massive blow to his head, and he was smashed forward onto the asphalt of the shared pathway. His first thought, in the instant before his face met the hard surface, was that he had been run into by a cyclist. Then, for a little while, there was nothing but a darkness filled with bright wandering stars.

He returned to a half-consciousness as he felt himself being dragged off the path. There was a thump as his body slumped face-down into a ditch, then rough voices.

"Get his wallet, quick!"

"Fuck it, there's only five bucks in here! Stupid old bastard!" There was a sudden agonising kick to his ribs and he screamed briefly before his face was pushed down into the soft mud, stifling him. He struggled to turn his face to one side in order to breathe, finally succeeded.

"Piss off, quick!" Then long silence.

There was a terrible pain in his head, and the wandering stars came back again. After a long, long while, he managed to push himself up onto his hands. He couldn't see, and had to wipe his hands across his eyes again and again before some vision returned. He struggled upright, held onto a tree. Desperately he tried to find his phone, but it seemed to have gone, along with his wallet. A wave of dizziness swamped over him, but he managed to stagger onto the pathway.

It was hot, too hot, and very bright. But not far away he could make out the short concrete tunnel where the shared pathway ran under a road. He knew it well, he had walked this way through the park for years.

He stumbled forward. Something wet was running down into his eyes, and he kept having to wipe it away. It took several eternities to reach the blessed shade of the tunnel.

There, among the broken beer bottles, he sat down gratefully and rested his head against the wall beneath the fantastic colours of the exuberant graffiti. Then there was a sudden surge of nausea, and he leaned over to one side to retch. Then he sank back, and his vision started to blur again. Someone would be along soon, they'd help. Then the darkness rose up and swallowed him.

A family group were the first to come along, a mother and two young children, all on bicycles.

"Oh, Mummy, look! There's a dirty old man here, and he's bleeding!"

"Come away, darling, get back on your bike. It's just an old drunk. Disgusting!"

And they cycled on.

The next people along the path were a middle-aged couple with a dog. The dog came up to where Brian lay unconscious, and sniffed at the vomit.

"Come away," snapped the man to the dog, yanking on its leash, but the woman came over and looked down, concerned.

"James, I think this man may be ill. Should we call an ambulance?"

The man shook his head in irritation. "We don't have time for all that. I've got to get ready for the evening service. He's all right, he wouldn't thank us for any fuss. Look at those beer bottles, he's just been drinking. I'll call the council in the morning and complain about how poorly these parks are maintained."

And they walked on.

Dozens of lycra-clothed cyclists zipped by, never pausing.

It was late now, and dusk started to settle over the park. Very few were about now on the path. But three teenagers ambled up, carrying spray cans and torches.

"Ah shit, there's some old guy here, just where I wanted to dress up my tag," said one.

"We can work around him," said another. "Hey, hey, why don't we do a white outline around him, you know, like on CSI?"

"Nah," said the third, and squatted down beside Brian's body. "He's been bashed up, I think. He's bleeding." He paused for a long time, thinking. "I think we should call an ambulance. Ring 911."

"Aw, shit, no. Besides, you mean triple-zero. You been watching too many of those American cop shows. But we don't want any of that shit. The cops'll think we bashed him."

"Not if we call them instead of pissing off. Besides, we don't need to call the cops, just an ambulance. We should help him. The Holy Koran says that to save one person is the same as saving all mankind."

"You been listening too much to your Imam. But… yeah, guess you're right."

The youth who had been squatting beside Brian stood up in decision. "Ditch the spray cans, hide 'em somewhere so we can find them again. Triple-zero, that right?"

He pulled out his phone and made the call.

Not All Those Who Wander

"Do be careful, dear," said Marian anxiously as her husband pulled abruptly away from the kerb to the accompaniment of a blaring horn and shouted curses from the taxi he had just cut off. Thank goodness here at the airport everyone was travelling quite slowly, she thought.

"Yes, yes," he said in annoyance, tightening his hands on the steering wheel. "These bloody young drivers have got no idea these days. No courtesy! No manners!" He glared angrily out at the world, much as he did when watching the television news every night.

"I think we need to turn just up there, Rob, see that sign?" She knew that he found it difficult driving at night, with all the glaring lights. But he had insisted on driving their daughter to the airport, despite Jane offering to get a taxi. He wouldn't hear of it. Terrible things happened to young women in taxis. Even though Jane was in her fifties now, and divorced. It made no difference. He was going to drive her.

Rob always insisted on things, and these days often flew into a rage if he was contradicted. Marian sighed. Now well into his eighties, Rob was becoming harder and harder to live with. Not that it had ever been easy. There had been plenty of fights while they were trying to make a go of their farm so many years ago. But she always remembered the golden-haired youth she had first fallen in love with, and she found that she could forgive him a great deal.

"Turn *here*, Rob," she said again, a little panicky because the turn was coming up quickly now. He made a grumpy sound, but swung the wheel over sharply, and they careered around the bend.

It was a long, long time since they had last been to the airport, and everything seemed to have changed. There were new roads, and lots more signs. Confusing signs. Gazing up at them as they drove along, Marian wasn't too sure herself which was the best way back home. She fumbled out the street directory. But her eyesight wasn't what it used to be, and the street lights and the shadows came and went over the book. She couldn't make any sense of it.

"It's this way," her husband said. He was peering out through his spectacles. "Blackwood, see," he said. Blackwood was the suburb where they lived now.

"No, Rob, it wasn't Blackwood, it was *Beechworth*. I'm sure... Oh, dear, I think we're getting on to the freeway."

Sure enough, they were passing under a green sign indicating the start of the freeway, and cars were zooming by them in the lane they needed to merge with. Rob was still travelling only at the suburban speed limit. "Oh, oh, Rob... you'd better speed up a little, dear."

He hunched down over the wheel, glaring at the speeding traffic. "Everyone travels too damn fast these days," he said.

She couldn't remember the last time they had driven on a freeway. They merged into the traffic, miraculously avoiding being driven into from the rear. Cars swerved out from behind them, horns blaring.

"They're going so fast because we're on the freeway, dear. I think we need to get off at the next exit."

"No, no, I know where we're going. This freeway will get us there faster, that's all."

She let out a long breath. "Please, Rob, I'm sure we're not going the right way."

"Damn it, I know what I'm doing, woman. Just trust me. Keep a lookout for a sign."

They passed several of the huge green signs, but none read "Blackwood".

Marian was starting to wish that they had let Jane buy them the navigation gadget she had talked about. But Marian was sure that they would have found it too hard to use. Jane was always worrying about them. The very last thing she had said to them at the airport was "Now do drive carefully, Dad. Just go back the way you came and you'll be all right."

But somehow they hadn't managed to get back on the road they had come on. Now Marian had no idea where they were. Rob was going a little faster now, but still not quite matching the speed of most of the freeway traffic. There was so *much* traffic, even at this time of night. *Where are all these people going?* she wondered. *Don't they have homes to go to?*

"Dear, I *really* think you had better take the next exit. Then we'll have a quiet look at the street directory and work out the best way to get home. We've gone quite a long way already."

Rob put on his stubborn face for a while and didn't reply. Then grudgingly, he said "I suppose you might be right. Look out for an exit, then."

One came up shortly, with a sign reading "Rochester. Exit 1 km."

"Um, you'd better slow down, Rob." He had gradually sped up to match the surrounding traffic, but now he needed to be prepared to stop.

"Stop your fussing, woman!"

But he did gradually ease off and diverged when she prompted him. They pulled up to a stop light at the end of the ramp. Marian bent down over the street directory again as Rob turned right when the light turned green. But he didn't pull over, as she had hoped, but just kept on driving.

Marian frowned down at the map book, turning over the pages desperately, to little effect. She looked up, trying to spot an unusual street name so she could look it up in the index, but all the streets here seemed to have very common names, and those she managed to look up, squinting, had dozens of entries.

"This way," Rob said, and turned left at the next major intersection. Marian had no idea on what basis he had made the decision. "But where...?" she asked.

"Damn it, just be quiet. I'll get us home."

She sighed again, and subsided back. They were on a wide, dual-carriage road, passing through a suburb full of similar-looking houses. Then they passed through a small shopping strip. She squinted out, trying to spot a surburb name on one of the businesses. But nothing made sense.

After a while, the road became narrower and narrower. Street lights were few and there were less houses.

"Rob, we're lost. We should pull over and ask somebody for directions."

He only grunted and kept on driving.

Marian looked at the dashboard clock and was shocked to realise that it was just after midnight. They had both been up early, and she was becoming very tired. She knew that Rob must be feeling the same way, and she kept glancing at him to make sure that he wasn't dropping off to sleep. That really would be awful.

"Rob, please, dear, we *must* stop and get some help."

"No, no, we're right now, I recognise the way."

Marian peered into the darkness. She couldn't see anything, let alone any landmarks.

"Rob..."

He just grunted. After a long, long while, he said, "Besides, there's no one to ask, see for yourself."

It was true. There were no street lights or house lights any more.

"I'll just keep going for a bit," he said. "We're bound to see a petrol station or something. We can ask there, if you're so fussed."

But there were no petrol stations. From time to time Rob's head drooped and then snapped upright again. Finally, Marian realised that she had to put her foot down.

"Rob, you *have* to stop. You're going to fall asleep at the wheel and we'll both be killed. Do you want me to be killed?"

"No, no," he said wearily, seeming to be quite confused now. "Where are we?"

"I don't know, Rob. But please pull over and stop."

"But..." he said, and tears glinted in his eyes. "What are we going to do? We can't sleep in the car."

"Yes we can," she said. "We've done it before, remember, when we were young?"

"Yes," he said faintly, as he pulled the car well off the asphalted road and turned it off. "Yes, I remember. Oh God, Marian, I'm so tired."

"Put your seat back, love. Just lie back. We'll find someone to help us in the morning."

"Yes, yes, you're right." He closed his eyes and lay back. After a moment he said, "I love you, Marian."

This, from Rob, was very rare. Fighting back her tears, she said quietly, "I love you too, Rob."

She put her own seat back and tried to go to sleep. It wasn't so easy. Rob began to snore, and it was a little cold in the car. It was pitch dark outside, with no moon. She could hear all kinds of little animal noises, snickerings and whistles. And the car seat, even tilted back, wasn't at all comfortable. Still, she eventually went to sleep, though she woke up several times. Rob finally seemed to have stopped snoring.

Marian was wakened at last by the morning sun. She opened her eyes and looked out her side window, away from the glare of the sun.

"Oh!" she said, "How lovely!"

Beyond a ploughed field, a beautiful green hill rose up high before her, delicately lit by the rising sun. It was densely planted with some kind of verdant crop, and textured with the path of a tractor. Birds sang brightly. Marian felt a deep sense of contentment after the anxiety of the night before. She felt truly at peace.

"Look, Rob," she said, turning to him, "isn't it…" Then she was silent.

Rob had stopped snoring in the night. And he had stopped breathing, too, she realised. She put her hand on his arm. It was startlingly cold.

"Oh Rob," she said, and sat quietly, holding his arm, crying a little. Then she turned back to the beautiful landscape. Just up ahead was a farmhouse. It didn't look too far for her to walk. She would do that presently. But not just yet.

"It's all right, Rob," she said, with a lump in her throat. "It's all right. You've brought us home."

Buddha Laughed

Robert waited for Kazuko in the park outside the Chinese restaurant, feeling stiff and foolish in his best suit. He had last worn it to his son's wedding.

As he waited, nervous, he kept looking at the stone statue which seemed to be guarding the path which led to the restaurant door. An absurdly fat man, with pendulous ear-lobes, laughing. Was it representing Buddha? He didn't know. It seemed too irreverent a figure to represent the figurehead of a major religion.

Here she came at last, her lean figure coming up the path from the river.

She came up to him, stood on her tiptoes and gave him a chaste peck on the cheek, which he received rather awkwardly.

"Sorry I'm late," she said, her eyes twinkling. He noted for the first time, being this close to her, that there were a few grey hairs beginning to be visible in her otherwise straight black hair.

"No, no, quite all right," he said. "Er... I've been entertaining myself looking at this fellow." He pointed to the statue. "Buddha, is it?"

Kazuko laughed. "Some call him the Laughing Buddha. In China they call him Pu-Tai, and in Japan we call him Hotei. A very popular fellow, always carrying a sack of goodies for children. Almost like an Asian Santa Claus, I guess. It's supposed to be good luck to rub his belly."

"I see," Robert said. "And he established Buddhism, did he?"

She laughed again. "Oh no! No, that's a common mistake Westerners make. Hotei was just a Buddhist monk in China in the 10th Century. The founder of Buddhism was Gautama Buddha, much, much earlier. Anyway," she said, "why are we standing here talking about Hotei? Let's go in."

"Just a sec," Robert said, and bent down to lightly rub the belly of the stone statue. Kazuko laughed yet again. He was starting to like that laugh.

As they were being seated at their table in the restaurant, Robert said "I'm surprised you suggested a Chinese restaurant and not a Japanese one."

"Oh, we can go to a Japanese restaurant another time. I thought you might enjoy Yum Cha for lunch. Have you had it before?"

He shook his head. "No. But I've had Chinese a few times," he said truthfully. Chinese take-away brought home by his son, he didn't say.

Another time, he was thinking. That at least sounded positive. But he would have to see how this meal panned out. He was so out of touch, so clumsy with women. He'd probably make some gross mistake, and that would be the end of it.

In fact, Kazuko had been forced to drop several heavy hints at the Adult Education Centre before he had realized that she was suggesting they go out together. He was doing an Advanced Photography course, and they had met in the Centre's canteen. Kazuko was teaching Basic Japanese.

He found her very attractive, though, of course, totally different from his late wife. Kazuko was dark and compact, a head shorter than him, with deep brown eyes, now set among a pattern of wrinkles. Goodness knows what she saw – if anything – in him. In comparison with Kazuko he felt awkward and gangling. And his hair was now entirely white.

The food began to arrive, in small bamboo steamers, all kinds of different little goodies. Desperately striving to make small talk he asked "So how long have you been in Australia?"

"Oh," she said with a smile, "about 52 years. I was born here. In Ballarat, actually."

"Oh God," he said. "I'm a fool." He could feel himself blushing.

She shook her head. "It's a very common mistake. My mother is an Australian. Blonde, would you believe? But I got all of my father's looks. They met in Japan when she was over there studying."

He was struggling with the chopsticks, trying to pick up the slippery dumplings from the steamer. Feeling very clumsy.

Kazuko collared a passing waiter. "Please bring the gentleman a fork and spoon," she said.

"Thanks. I… I need more practice."

"So I can see. It's easy for me, of course. Have you ever seen one of those martial arts movies where the hero catches a passing fly with his chopsticks? No? Well, I'm not quite *that* good."

She talked for a little about her family and about growing up as a Japanese child in Ballarat in the 1960?s and 70?s. "I was a bit of an outsider when I started at school, of course," she said. "Kids always want to bully someone different from themselves. But I eventually found that developing a sense of humour, turning the gibes off with a joke, that helped a lot."

"Now," she said. "Tell me something about yourself."

Awkwardly, he managed to outline some of his life, careful not to bore her with too much detail. Growing up in Adelaide, studying to become a draftsman, his struggle to make the transition to computer-aided drafting before moving into administration.

"Now they are trying to push me into retiring," he said sadly. "I suppose I can afford to, but I don't know what I would do with myself. It would be different if Pat was still alive. We'd go travelling abroad, I guess, but there's not much fun in travelling by yourself, or on one of those dreadful packaged tours."

"But you are keen on photography?"

"Well, I'm trying to get better at it. That's why I'm doing the course at the AEC. I used to do quite a bit when I was young. I had my own darkroom. But it's all changed so much now with digital. I'm having to learn it all again."

"In fact," he said slowly, "the class has organized a photo-walk around the Botanical Gardens next week. I... I wonder if you would like to come along?"

"Of course," she said with a smile. "I'll look forward to it."

After a mild wrangle about the bill – Robert insisted on paying – they parted outside, next to the statue. She gave Robert a rather less chaste kiss than before, and headed off to catch her train.

Robert looked down at Hotei and patted him on the head.

"Thanks," he said.

At the End of His Tether

He'd left a note, of course. It was quite brief, but at the end he'd asked his neighbour -- begged her, really -- to look after Sally. Mrs Donovan loved dogs, had two of her own. Sally would fit right in. He didn't have to worry about that at least.

He'd bought the rope at the hardware store in Hannover Street. Four metres should be more than enough. The shop assistant hadn't asked him any questions. No reason she should, really. He wasn't a regular there, didn't do much in the way of home maintenance.

Back home, in his kitchen, he tried to tie a proper hangman's knot. He'd looked it up on the Internet, actually. Amazing what you could find out on the Internet. Except for a reason to go on living, of course. You could Google that phrase, but all that came back was predictable religious-oriented hog-wash, 300 million hits. All empty, meaningless, like his life.

Except for Sally, that is. She'd kept him going longer than he'd thought possible after Jenny had died. But there were limits on how much comfort a dog's companionship could give you. And now he'd reached that limit.

The knot was tied. He'd made a bit of a mess of it, really. It didn't look much like the drawing he'd found online. Typical of how he'd botched most things in his life. Still, the loop moved freely enough. It would do.

Sally was in her basket in the corner, looking up at him eagerly. She probably thought he was going to take her out for a walk. "Not tonight, sweetheart." Never again, actually. Not that Sally knew that, of course. Although now she was whining and looking at him, staring deeply at him. She knew something was wrong.

He should put her outside, but it was cold out there and in a while it would be getting dark. And she'd have to stay out there all night, maybe longer. Who could tell how long it would be before they found him, and Mrs Donovan read the note? But if he left her inside... That could be worse. What if it took a week? Mrs Donovan might realise that she hadn't seen him for a while, but surely not straight away.

He hadn't thought things through, obviously. He'd been too wound up in his own misery, he'd only been able to focus on his one mission, a way to bring it all to an end.

Sally whined again. In a sudden rush of resolution, he hardened his heart, stood up with the rope, and stepped through the door into the lounge room, closing it behind him firmly before Sally could follow him. In the lounge room there was an angled ceiling which followed the shape of the roof. At intervals where the cross-beams ran, there was a space between the cedar beams and the ceiling itself, enough room to fit the rope. He'd been staring at those gaps for weeks, thinking about it. This was where he was going to do it. He stood up on the table and threaded the free end of the rope through.

Sally started to bark, and leap up at the door in the kitchen. He could hear her claws clattering and dragging down the wood. She'd never done that before. He tried to close his mind to the sound, but it didn't work.

Suddenly, standing there stupidly on the table, the noose dangling from his hand, he found that he couldn't shut out thoughts about what would happen to Sally without him. Would Mrs Donovan really take her in? She was on a pension, he knew. Feeding an extra dog might be too much.

She's just a stupid dog, he thought savagely to himself. *What does it matter if she's taken to the pound, given away to some cruel stranger, or put down? Just a damn dog! A damn dog! She doesn't matter. But then, but then...*

The barking was frantic now. *She loves you,* he thought. *There's still one creature in the world who you matter to, who values your life. And she does matter. She matters a lot.*

He stood there on the table for a long, long time. After a while, he dropped the noose and climbed foolishly down.

He opened the kitchen door. "Come on, girl," he said in a husky voice he could hardly identify as his own. "Let's go for a walk."

Slow Dawn

Gasping for breath, Paul bent over to rest his hands on his knees, allowing him a reprieve from the weight of his backpack for a precious moment or two. He looked upward at the slope ahead of him.

He was starting to think that coming on this bushwalk with the others had been a big mistake. He wasn't as fit as he had thought he was, and it was hot, hot, too damned hot. Sweat was dripping from his head and running into his eyes. He pulled out his water bottle and took a sip. There wasn't much left. Shane and Berndt said that there was probably – *probably!* – a water tank in the hut at the top of the mountain.

Mount Dreadful wasn't all *that* high, Paul supposed. Not much of a mountain at all by international standards. It had looked OK on the map Shane had shown him. Mind you, he hadn't thought to count the contour lines or see how closely packed they were. As it was, ever since leaving the cars parked at the foot of the slope just after lunch, they had been walking up a continuous slope. Paul had lost all sense of how far up they had come, or how far they still had to go. Surrounded by trees, there was no way to get a bearing, even if his map-reading skills had been more than rudimentary.

Sighing, he set off again, trying to push the pace just a little in order to catch up.

Around the next corner the path was blocked by the thick trunk of a gum tree which must have fallen recently. Leaning against the trunk, waiting for him, was Marina.

Marina was Shane's girlfriend. She was also the secret reason that Paul had agreed to come on this bushwalk. His heart gave a painful twang when he saw her, and at the same time he felt a wave of self-disgust. *How feeble I must seem to her*, he thought.

"Come on, Paul!" Marina said cheerfully. "You can do it."

Paul forced his eyes away from Marina and looked up the slope. "How far ahead..?"

"Oh, I don't know," she said with a laugh. "I've given up trying to catch them. Shane and Berndt are trying to out-do each other. And Berndt has this rotten habit of sprinting ahead, then waiting for you to catch up, and then heading off again just as you get there. Do you want a drink?"

"Thanks, but I've got my own water bottle." He shook it, and it was obvious that there wasn't much left.

"Have some of mine. It's a bigger bottle than yours, and I haven't been drinking so much."

"No..." He didn't want to feel too indebted to her.

"Come on, you'll relieve me of the weight. And if you don't drink, you'll never make it to the top."

So he took her bottle gratefully and drank a big swig of water. Handing it back, he said "Can we get around this tree?"

"Nope, it's wedged in here, and the bush is too dense to get around. It's not too hard to climb up and across, though." And she demonstrated. Paul looked at her lithe brown legs as she climbed and sighed inwardly yet again.

He followed, and for a long while they toiled up the slope together, not speaking. But he took some comfort from the temporary feeling of companionship with her. So close, but so out of reach.

They both had to stop several times to rest. Paul emptied his water bottle, and accepted another gulp from Marina's, under protest. "Drink!" she commanded. Then they went on again.

Finally, the tree cover started to diminish as they reached what would be the snow line in winter. Then there were no trees at all and soon they were walking along a bare dusty trail which started to level off as they reached the peak.

They saw the fire-spotter's tower first. A tall framework tower with a narrow ladder leading up to an enclosed platform at the top. Then, as they came closer, they saw the old rustic shepherd's hut which had been repaired and expanded over the years by the rangers of the Parks Service, for the benefit of bushwalkers like themselves.

Shane and Berndt were sitting on the veranda of the hut, waiting for them. Berndt had been born in Germany, and on bushwalks he donned the same outfit he would wear back in Europe. He looked the part of an Alpine shepherd, in leather pants and suspenders, right out of *The Sound of Music*. You expected him to be quaffing beer out of a pottery stein. But there was no beer.

"Is there water?" Paul croaked out. Shane nodded. "Tank's full," said.

Paul knocked on the side of the corrugated-iron water tank which collected rainwater. It rang with a heavy, full sound. The best sound in the world. Worth a million dollars to Paul right then. Gratefully he found the tap and filled up his water bottle, drank most of it down, then filled it again. He sat down in contentment. Well, as much contentment as he could manage, given that Shane and Marina were now sitting cuddling on the veranda.

There was some debate about their plans. Berndt wanted to push on, down the other side of the mountain and along a river trail, but it was now late afternoon, mostly due to how long it had taken Paul and Marina to reach the top. Marina objected, to Paul's relief, and insisted that it would be far more sensible to stay the night in the hut. Shane seemed indifferent, and after some grumbling Berndt agreed.

There were a couple of small rooms in the hut. Shane and Marina claimed one of the rooms where they could lay down their sleeping bags, which were designed to allow them to be zipped together into a double bag. Paul shied away from thinking about that and put his own sleeping bag down in the other room.

Berndt, the iron man, declared that he would sleep out on the veranda. Paul half-expected him to declare that he would do it without a sleeping bag, naked.

They made a fire in an established stone-ringed fireplace outside the hut – it was still outside the formal bushfire season and as yet there was no fire ban. They cooked the food they had brought with them – in Berndt's case some actual steak, now looking just a little green from the heat of the day, but cooking up well enough after a rinse in tank water. Shane and Marina shared a package of tuna and noodles. Paul reconstituted some dehydrated vegetable soup.

The truth was, Paul thought, that he hadn't been at all well prepared for this walk. It was his first real bushwalk, in fact, and he had just cobbled together what equipment and supplies he could. The others had all been walking together before. While Paul had been on short day-walks before with Shane, it had been over relatively level ground, nothing like the terrible endless slope they had endured today.

And so to bed. He lay awake for a time, dreading hearing sounds of love-making from the room next door, but in fact there was silence.

He spent an uncomfortable, cold night. His cheap sleeping bag wasn't very efficient, and didn't keep him warm against the freezing mountain air. He did catch some snatches of sleep, though, and woke to hear Berndt putting on his boots out on the veranda. Curious, Paul shrugged out of his bag and went to look.

There was the barest glimmer of light in the east. Berndt looked up and said "I'm going off to do a side-walk down the little valley down there. I'll be back for breakfast in an hour or two."

"OK," Paul said. Nothing on earth would have induced him to do any extra walking. His calves and thighs were stiff and painful from the previous day's walk.

As Berndt marched off into the semi-darkness, Paul sat down on the veranda and watched the slow brightening in the eastern sky. There was a cloud-bank, and slowly the clouds began to light up from underneath in colours of salmon and orange.

He heard a sound from behind him, and looked up in surprise to see Marina. "Shane's snoring," she said, "so I thought I would get up to see the dawn." She sat down beside Paul and they watched the pro-gressive illumination of the sky, which became a spectacular blaze of red and orange with hints of purple.

"It's beautiful," she said softly.

"So are you," Paul said without thinking.

Then he realised what he had let out and slapped his palm across his mouth in horror. "Oh, God! I'm sorry, I..."

She looked at him with a beatific smile. "It's OK," she said. "Thanks."

Paul's heart was still dropping within him, it seemed like it was sinking into the depths. "I shouldn't have... I... you're with Shane."

"Yes," she said firmly, standing up, but still smiling. "I am." She turned to go back into the hut, then stopped and gave Paul an amused look. "But who knows, I might not *always* be." And winked, and was gone.

Paul looked back at the spectacular dawn, a slow glimmer of hope rising in him along with the sun.

A new day began.

The Fire of the Gods

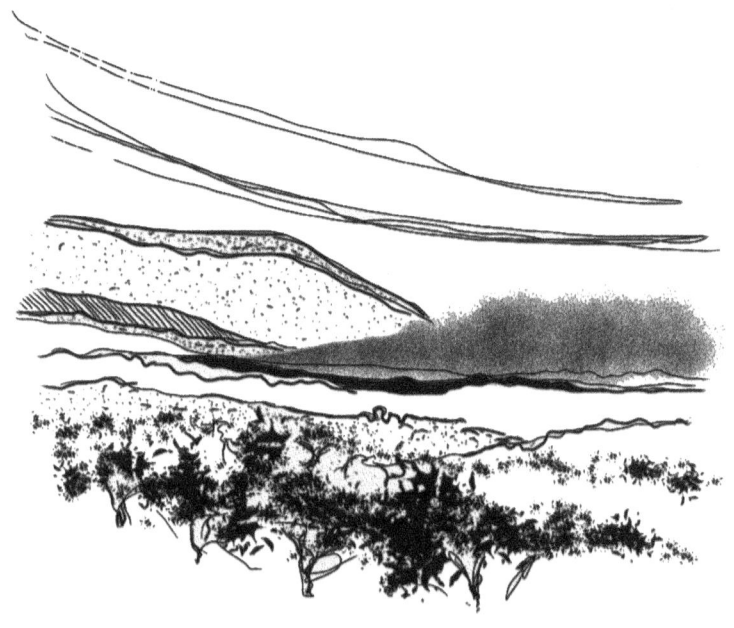

The hammering on his door came as no surprise. He'd been expecting it. It was about the fire, of course.

He'd always been fascinated by fire. When he was very young, living in cold England, he spent hours watching the coal burn in the grate, made up fantastic stories about castles of burning flame, volcanoes and avalanches of red-hot rocks.

When he was older he had been constantly in trouble for playing with matches. In his bedroom, he made a secret place to hide away matches and candles. He carried out endless experiments as he applied the flames to anything he could find. He'd melted many a toy soldier, set alight countless scraps of cloth, cooked morsels of food or animal hair. Sometimes the stench was sickening.

When he was denied matches, he would read. He loved to read, grabbed up anything interesting he could find in the local library. Stories, of course, but also books on myths and legends. Especially anything which mentioned fire. So he discovered the story of Prometheus, who had stolen fire from the gods and given it to mankind. And that was right and proper, he thought. Fire belonged to humans. Fire was the tool which freed people from cold, transformed their food, shaped their tools, and drove their engines.

In high school his favourite subject was chemistry. The fierce blue flame of the bunsen burner was his delight. He set fire, unauthorised, to sulphur and gloried in its choking blue flame until it drove all of the students from the laboratory. Then there was magnesium ribbon. Setting fire to magnesium created a blinding white light which travelled slowly along the ribbon, emitting clouds of white smoke. He stole a whole reel of it but was caught.

There were some more incidents. One night a whole wing of the school caught fire and burned down. He had enjoyed that a lot. Suspicions were aroused, but the police couldn't prove anything.

Not long after, his parents decided to emigrate to Australia. His father had always wanted to go there, and the suspicions about the fire were another incentive to seek a new environment.

Before they left, he read up on everything he could find about Australia. To his intense excitement, he found that it was a land literally shaped by fire. The whole ecology had evolved, not merely to cope with frequent fires, but to *depend* upon them. There were trees with seeds which would only sprout once they had been burned, trees whose bark peeled off in long dry strips, all the better to create fuel. It would be, for him, a paradise.

He completed school in Australia but his academic performance was poor, and he was unable to progress to university, something which distressed his parents but not himself. He left home soon afterwards, staying in a squalid shared house with some young men of his own age, living on the dole and the occasional casual labouring job.

He spent a long time looking for the kind of job he wanted, and found it at last. A storeman with a laboratory supplies company. It was perfect. Cautiously, he started to siphon off small quantities of the things he loved. Sulphur. Magnesium. Gas cylinders. Anything inflammable. He paid for a small self-storage facility, which he visited regularly.

The shared house burned down one night a couple of years later. The men he lived with had been out. So had he, he claimed. The police questioned him, but there was no evidence of arson. He had learned how to cover his traces. No stupid splashing around of petrol. A small flame applied in the right place, and *patience*, was all it took.

By then he had saved some money. It hadn't been hard, as he spent very little. Girls held no interest for him. Fire was better than sex, and anyway few young women showed an interest in him. He moved out to the country, taking with him his stores. He found another job, and soon had enough for a deposit on a ramshackle old house on the edge of a forest. With the trees that loved fire.

He joined the local volunteer fire service and enjoyed the drills, attended a few fires and helped put them out. Most of all he enjoyed burn-offs, where he was actually *directed* to light small fires to burn off the leaf litter and underbrush before it could become dangerous. But these were tame affairs, and always the fires had to be put out too quickly for his liking.

His reluctance in this regard started to attract attention, and he quit the team.

Then came the big fire. It was a frighteningly hot day, well over 40 degrees Celsius, with the wind gusting strongly from the north. A Total Fire Ban was declared. He was quietly outraged. You couldn't banish fire that way.

The bushfire that day was appalling in its result. From a small initial blaze on the outskirts of town, it expanded rapidly into an unstoppable firestorm. By the time it died out, hundreds of homes had been destroyed and dozens of lives had been lost.

They came for him the next day, and he was waiting. He had everything ready. When the knocking and yelling began, he lit the fuses. With the bushfire, he had almost achieved his peak. The house would be his ultimate triumph.

His home-made magnesium flares went off first, almost blinding the crowd outside, and scattering them. Then the petrol containers erupted into fireballs on either side of the house, and gas cylinders started to explode. He stood in the lounge room, waiting as the fire blossomed nearer and then reached him. Waiting eagerly. And then the pain engulfed him.

He had burned himself in small ways many times and thought he had been ready for the pain. He had thought that fire was his friend, that the gift of fire came from heaven, from the gods. But he was wrong.

Too late he realised that instead, it came from hell.

Under the Pump

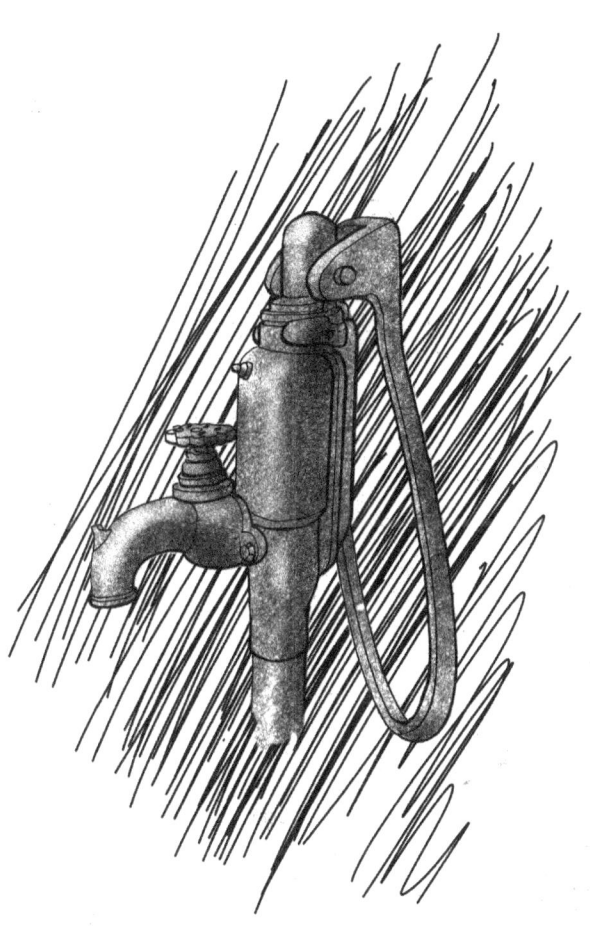

Alan Holdsworth paced around the office, checking on his staff at their desks. Everyone was under pressure. "How's it going, John?" he asked a young man feverishly typing at his workstation.

"Same as before," John said with only mild irritation. "I'll be at least another hour, and then Tara has to lay it all out. Does Bob have the figures done?"

"He's still working on them," Alan said. He checked his watch. It was nearly six-thirty. "I'd better give my wife a call."

The phone rang for a long while, and for a while Alan thought that Helen wouldn't answer, but at last she picked up.

"Sorry, babe," he said. "I'm going to be late again."

"So what's new?" came her cool voice. "Is it the blonde this time, or the brunette?"

"No, no, nothing like that. We're really under the pump trying to get this tender submission out. Beckham Industries. Due in before 9 am tomorrow."

"Under the pump, again. Seems to me you're always under the pump." Though her words were sharp, she didn't seem too annoyed. Still, probably time for him to show a bit more interest, he thought.

"So what have you been up to today, Hel?"

"Oh," she said, "this and that. Clearing a few things out. Been rearranging the furniture. Not sure you'll like the new layout, but I do. So what time do you think you'll be back?"

"Bit hard to tell. Could be late. I'll send you a text when I'm leaving."

"OK. I will be gone for a bit myself." And she put the phone down.

Alan returned to prowling the office, hovering over one workstation after another. He couldn't do much to contribute to the tender, though he did proof-read the copy and gave a quick check of the figures in the quote. Then he went to check on Tara's layout, which was only preliminary as she waited for final content from the others in the team.

"Sorry to put you under the pump," he said to Tara, as she laid things out on her large monitor.

Tara was from the States, and she glanced at him in irritation. "What the hell does *that* mean?"

"Under pressure, pushing to meet a deadline. It must be an Aussie expression. Maybe it's something to do with sticking your head under a water pump to cool down when you've been working hard."

Tara just compressed her lips and kept working. Hard.

Eventually, hours later, it was all done. It would be dropped into the tender box in the morning before the deadline by Bob, who lived in a city apartment nearby.

Alan went down to the garage and started his car. He checked his watch. Ten-thirty. He picked up his phone and stabbed out a quick text.

on the way home now see you

The response came back quickly, but it was puzzling.

not if I see you first

There wasn't much traffic at that time of night, and it only took him about a half hour to drive home to his suburban house. It wasn't a huge house, but it was in a good suburb, and if he got a promotion or two at the office they would be able to extend, make room for kids.

He frowned as he pulled into his driveway. Helen could at least have left the porch light on for him, he thought. He picked up his briefcase and went to the door. Helen must be asleep, there were no lights on. He turned his key in the lock and went in.

There was an odd feel to the house as he stepped from the hallway into the lounge. He switched on the light. He gave a gasp with the sudden shock and then dropped his briefcase with a thud.

Helen had been rearranging the furniture, all right. It was all gone. The lounge was completely cleared, empty of everything except the carpet. Even the drapes were missing.

As he stood there gaping, his phone gave a bing. Dazedly, he pulled it out and read the text message.

welcome home. lol

He fumbled three letters and a punctuation mark:

wtf?

But there was no immediate reply.

He went from room to room, turning on lights as he went. They were all bare, every one. Pale patches on the walls where the paintings and framed photographs had been. Finally he came to the kitchen. It, too, was bare of furniture. But leaning drunkenly in the sink was a rusty old water pump. He had last seen it at the farm Helen's father owned.

His phone binged again. She must be somewhere nearby, watching him, he realized, tracking his progress by the lights he had turned on. He looked at the message.

> *i got you your very own pump maybe you can install it in the shower? bye*

The Broomstick Party

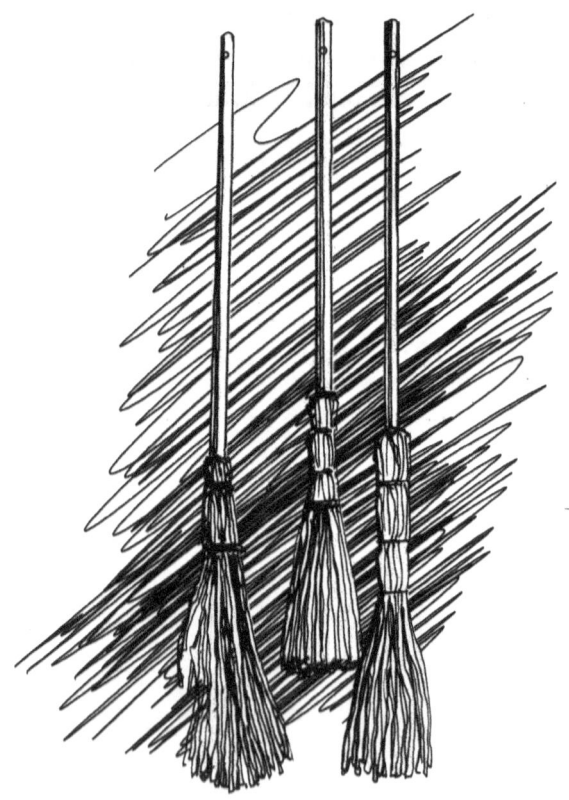

"I've got a secret," Jessica whispered proudly to her cousin Leah. "You'll find out later."

Leah, who was staying for the weekend for the first time at Jessica's new house, pouted a little, but really only because Jessica would expect it. "Tell me, tell me now!" she said.

"Not here," Jessica said. "Bring your bag and come up to my room." Leah dutifully picked up her backpack and followed Jessica up the stairs.

"So this is it," said Jessica as they entered the pink and floral room. "You get to sleep on this," she said, pulling out the low trundle bed from beneath her own. "It's not bad, I tried it out last night."

Leah looked around. Even at eight years old she knew enough to be a little disgusted by the pink frilliness of Jessica's room, with its soft toys and posters of unicorns. Her own bedroom was filled with a haphazard mess of construction toys and electronics, decorated in bright primary colors with posters of rock bands that her mother regularly demanded she take down.

"Very nice," she said insincerely. "Now, come on, tell me your secret!"

Jessica smirked. "It's the old lady next door. *She's a witch!*"

"Oh, really?" Leah said sceptically. "How do you know?"

"I've been watching her ever since we moved in here. She lives all by herself in that run-down house, see?" Jessica pointed out the window at the house next door, which did indeed look in need of repair. It looked as if it had been there for a very long time. Maybe it was the original farmhouse, before all the land around it had been sold and new houses put up?

"So what?" Leah said, unwilling to show Jessica any excitement. "So she lives by herself."

"*And* she always dresses in black, never anything else. *And* she talks in a funny language, to herself. I heard her one day in the street. I think she's reciting spells. *And* she has a black cat. Well, two, actually, and one of them is just grey, but the other one is really black. See, there it is!"

Leah nodded. "OK, sounds interesting. Anything else?"

"I'm *coming* to the best bit. I sneaked in her back yard one day when she was out. And I saw... no. I'm not going to tell you, you'll just have to see. Tomorrow morning. She goes out nearly every morning."

And no matter how hard Leah pressed her, Jessica wouldn't say any more about the witch that day. They had dinner and watched a scary movie. Well, Jessica screamed a lot, so Leah figured that it must be scary, but she herself saw most of the frights coming ages before they happened.

In the morning, Jessica bounced out of bed at eight o'clock. Leah was only half awake, as the girls had talked late into the night, despite being repeatedly shushed by Jessica's mother.

Jessica's parents had gone off shopping for the morning, leaving the girls to their own devices. They had a quick breakfast and then Jessica said, "We'll have to put on our exploring clothes. Did you bring some, like I said?"

Leah had. An old pair of jeans and a camouflage T-Shirt.

Together the girls changed and then looked out of the window at the old house next door. "See, there she goes."

Leah saw an old woman with an impressively wrinkled face, dressed all in black, hobbling down the path to the street, leaning on a stick. "See, that's her wand, I'll bet," Jessica said. "Come on, you've really got to see this!"

They left Jessica's house, and Jessica led Leah to the far end of the yard, which fronted onto a creek. By squirming around the last fence-post without slipping into the creek – not so easy, Leah got her feet wet – they found themselves in the old woman's yard.

In the yard, close to the house, was a rustic shed, all put together with roughly cut pieces of wood. Jessica was about to run up the yard towards it, but Leah stopped her. "Let's crawl along like commandos," she said. "So as not to be seen." Jessica looked dubious, but dutifully squirmed along the grass on her elbows with Leah. It was a bit silly, really, Leah admitted to herself, since no one was home but the two cats. But it was fun.

They reached the old shed. There wasn't even a door, just an opening. Jessica stood up and beckoned Leah inside. "Ta-DAH!" she said, waving at the wall.

There was a rack of honest-to-goodness broom-sticks of various shapes and sizes, all made of twigs and knobbly bits of bamboo. Oh, and a modern-looking bamboo garden rake.

Leah was really impressed. "Wow," she said. And a moment later, "Do you think they work? Does she fly around on them?"

"Of course she does, every time there's a full moon!"

"Really? Have you seen her?"

Jessica looked abashed. "Well, no, but it stands to reason, doesn't it?"

"And why does she need more than one?"

"Well, maybe she just likes trying out different ones. My dad always wants to try out different cars."

"Hmmm…" said Leah, and then, with a wicked grin, "*We* could try them out!"

Jessica went pale. Leah was fascinated, she had never see someone actually do that before. "Oh no," she said. "We… I mean, *what if it worked*?"

"Well, duh, that would be the whole point. Come on!" And Leah pulled down one of the broomsticks, gave it to Jessica, and then took another for herself.

Despite her initial hesitation, Jessica soon got into the spirit of the thing. The girls ran around the yard for quite some time, straddling the old broomsticks and shouting out whatever magical words they could think of. They didn't get a centimetre off the ground, but wore themselves out laughing.

Jessica had become quite excited, red in the face. "I know," she said, "we need to get a bit of a start. Look!"

At the other side of the yard was a rusty old oil drum, lying on its side. Jessica picked up a flat board from nearby and rested it on the top of the drum. Then she mounted the broomstick and started to run towards the board, bristles dragging over the grass.

Leah suddenly had a bad feeling. "Jessica, don't..."

Jessica ran onto the board, but instead of it acting as a ramp and letting her fly off into space, it broke under her weight, and twisted as she fell. Jessica came down sideways onto the drum, then rolled over it head first.

Leah ran over as Jessica began to scream. It was mostly fright, Leah thought as she checked out the other girl, but Jessica howled and held onto her ankle, which was grazed and had twisted as she had fallen. It was already starting to swell.

Just as Leah was wondering what to do, there was a noise from the house, and she looked up in alarm. The old woman was coming out of the back door of her house. The girls must have been playing with the broomsticks for a lot longer than they thought and she'd come back home.

Seeing the old lady, Jessica began to scream in fright and tried to get to her feet to run away, but it was impossible. "The witch, the witch," she moaned as she sank down again.

Leah stood up and faced the woman, who was hobbling nearer. Despite herself, Leah found that her knees were trembling. "I'm really, really sorry," she said, "I know we shouldn't have been here."

But instead of yelling (or turning them into frogs), the old lady just smiled and shook her head. "*Non fa niente, non importa*," she said. She bent down to Jessica, who tried to squirm away, but the old lady rested her hand on Jessica's leg and made soothing noises. "*Ah, poverina ragazza. Devo chiamare un'ambulanza?*" She had a kind voice that calmed Jessica down.

Leah understood the last word the old lady had said. Ambulance. Did Jessica need an ambulance? Well, no, thought Leah. She probably just needed to get back home and have a bandage put on. She tried to explain to the old lady that Jessica's parents weren't home, but that she would probably be OK without an ambulance.

"*Si, si. Aiutami,*" she said, gesturing at Jessica, who had finally stopped sobbing. "'elp me, inside *la casa*. The... the 'ouse."

Leah understood and helped Jessica up and supported her as she hopped towards the old lady's house. As they went, Jessica whispered "Leah? Is it OK? She's not going to hurt us?"

"No, I'm sure it's fine. She's not really a witch, you know, that was just a game we were playing."

Jessica nodded, but looked unconvinced. Inside the house, though, the old lady sat them down at her wooden kitchen table, whose surface was worn into soft shallows and grooves by long scrubbing. The old lady went to a cupboard and brought out an ancient looking pot with a lime-green paste in it, which she started to spread over Jessica's ankle. Jessica looked across at Leah as if to say "See – magic potion!". But then the old lady went back to the same cupboard and brought out a thoroughly modern-looking first aid box and wrapped a bandage around Jessica's ankle, finishing off with a small safety pin. "*Tutto fatto!*" she said with a smile.

"Um, thank you," said Jessica hesitantly.

"*E ora…,*" the old woman said, and went to a different cupboard, bringing back a large tin. She set it down on the table and opened it up. It was full of lots of different kinds of biscuits. Jessica again flashed a dubious look at Leah.

"Don't worry," said Leah, by now really enjoying herself, and taking a spiky-looking brown biscuit, "we can always shove her into her oven."

Jessica laughed, and took a biscuit herself. Leah bit into hers. It was delicious. "What is this called?" she asked the old woman.

The old lady laughed. "*Brutto ma buono,* 'ow you say, ah 'ugly but good'."

After several biscuits and a large glass of milk each, Jessica helped Leah up to take her home. Just as they went out the front door, they saw Jessica's parents drive up in their car. Surprised, the grown-ups stopped outside the old lady's house and got out to fuss over Jessica's injury. Many explanations and expressions of gratitude followed.

But as Jessica's parents were helping her back to their house, though, the old lady leaned over to Leah and whispered in her ear:

"About the ah… *il manico di scopa*… 'ow you say," she made a sweeping motion.

"The broomsticks? Yes, I'm sorry…"

"No. I tell you…" The old lady concentrated hard on saying what she meant in English. "When you ride 'im, you wrong. Wrong way round. *Le setole*… the bristles? They go at the front, OK?" And she winked.

"OK," said Leah faintly as the old lady turned back into the house. "Um, thanks, I'll remember."

Good Tidings

"I can't stand it any more," Luke said.

He and Mee Ying stood together at the counter, looking out at the endless flood of miserable faces as the crowds of people shuffled by, their expressions hollow, exhausted.

"What? This job?" Mee Ying asked.

"No, the damned music. If I hear that awful woman sing 'Oh Christmas Tree' one more time I'll go beserk, I promise you. Grab an axe and start smashing everything in sight."

She chuckled. "We don't have an axe."

"There's one in the corridor, for use in a fire. 'Break this glass'. I reckon this is close enough to an emergency to qualify."

Mee Ying laughed, and turned away to serve another customer. Luke sold someone a complete set of 'Friends' on HD Blu-Ray. Meanwhile, the endless Christmas music wound on and on: loud, sickly sweet and insincere.

"Can't we do something about it?" he said to Mee Ying the next time they both were free from customers. "Doesn't the music drive you crazy too?"

She sighed. "Yes, of course. But there's nothing we can do. Mr Pando likes it, says it creates the right Christmas spirit."

Mr Pando was the local store manager. His name wasn't really Pando, Luke knew. It was something Italian or Greek, Luke seemed to remember. Pandolfino or Pandolopulus or something like that. He was content to be called just Mr Pando. Luke wondered if he knew that all the female staff called him 'Handy-Pandy', with good reason.

"But Pando's only down in the store for five minutes every couple of hours. He doesn't have to put up with it. You know, I don't reckon Jesus ever wanted all of this," Luke said, waving his hand at the harrassed crowd of shoppers.

"Don't ask me," Mee Ying said, "I'm a Buddhist."

"Excuse me, do you have André Rieu's 'Home for Christmas Volume 3'?" a harried looking young woman in a dark pantsuit asked Luke. He looked at her with a raised eyebrow. "It's for my grandmother," the young woman explained testily.

Luke shook his head. "We only have movies and TV shows here," he said. "All the music videos are sold by the music department over on the other side of the store." He pointed.

The young woman made an annoyed sound. "How stupid. Why can't they put everything together?"

He shrugged. "That's the way management wanted it, I'm sorry." She turned away in

annoyance and stalked off.

On the audio system, 'Oh Christmas Tree' started up again. The woman singing it sounded as if she had a list of fifty more Christmas songs to go and she didn't think she was being paid enough to sing even one of them. Luke gritted his teeth, but didn't go to fetch the axe. Then the singer switched to the German version. "Oh Tannenbaum, O Tannenbaum…" It was not an improvement.

He looked at his watch. "Time for my break," he said. "Can you hold the fort for a few minutes?" The crowd had slacked off a little.

"Break?" she said, a little outraged. "Mr Pando cancelled…"

"Yeah, yeah," he said. "I'll only be a tick. Need to do something."

He trotted quickly off the shop floor and headed up to the next level. The toilets were here, but that wasn't where he was headed. He looked both ways to check there was no one watching, then ducked into a small room on the other side of the corridor.

There was a rack of computer and telephony equipment here, and also the hi-fi system, with a CD player, set to loop endlessly. He pushed the eject button, grabbed the CD, and pushed the tray back. He slid the CD on top of the tall server rack, well out of sight.

But as he stepped out of the equipment room into the corridor, he almost bumped into Mr Pando, coming out of the men's toilet. Mr Pando looked at Luke suspiciously, his florid face creased in a frown. "What were you doing in there?"

Luke thought quickly. "Um… there seemed to be something wrong with the Christmas CD, kept sticking. I think maybe it's been scratched somehow. But I… I gave it a clean and put it back, seems OK now. And, er, I needed to go to the loo."

Mr Pando nodded and then smiled. "I see. Well, thanks for that. It's wonderful to make sure everyone has the Christmas spirit, isn't it?" And he headed back to his office. A secretary coming in the other direction dodged well out of his way.

Luke, cursing inwardly, popped into the toilet for form's sake, waited a moment or two, then came back out and begrudgingly reinstated the CD into the player, but not before carefully scratching a small part of it with the end of a key.

Back on the shop level, a syrupy version of 'O Come All Ye Faithful' was playing, the first track on the CD. Enough to make all the faithful run away in the opposite direction, he thought. As he passed a middle-aged couple, he heard the woman say "Oh dear, I thought for a moment they had stopped that awful music, but now it's back again." The man nodded gloomily.

Mee Ying had a queue of three people waiting to be served. She frowned at him. "Sorry," he said, turning to serve the next customer in line.

Twenty minutes later the sound crackled and popped and started to repeat a short fragment. The player had reached the scratch Luke had made. He picked up the house phone and rang Pando's office.

"That CD's definitely defective, Mr Pando" he said. "Perhaps we should just turn it off?"

"No, no," Pando said. "It's not a problem, I have another CD here. Good to have some variety in any case. I'll go and put it in."

Five minutes later, André Rieu started up with vast over-orchestration. 'Silent Night' had never been less silent.

Luke groaned and Mee Ying laughed again. He liked her laugh. "Well, at least it's different," she said.

But by the end of their long shift, Luke had had more than enough of André Rieu, too. He decided that he needed a better plan. There were, after all, still three weeks until Christmas.

"Mee Ying," he said as they headed towards the doors, "your brother's a bit of an electronics nut, isn't he?"

"I don't know what you mean by 'nut'. He's studying computer science and electrical engineering, yes."

"Do you think he could rig something up for me? Something to fix the music player?" He explained his plan.

She smiled. "You are very wicked, Luke. But I'm sure Hoa could help. He loves building things like that. I'll give him a call. It's a bit late, but he stays up until after midnight most days."

She rang her brother, spoke briefly in Chinese and then handed her phone over to Luke. He repeated his plan.

"Sure!" said Hoa. "Won't be too hard, sounds like a lot of fun. I'll have to charge you for the parts, but it won't be much. I've just bought this little micro-processor kit which should do the trick with a few extra components. Take me a couple of days, maybe. But I'll have to come and help you wire it up, I think."

Two nights later, after another couple of dreary shifts behind the counter, Luke met Mee Ying's brother outside the store as the employees were leaving. He was a lean young man with a bright expression. They shook hands as Mee Ying introduced them. "I'll leave you boys to it," she said. "I'm exhausted."

The two young men went back inside and made their way up to the equipment room.

"Mr Pando – that's the boss – has left, he never stays late," Luke explained. "We've got about a half an hour before the cleaners start work, not that they would worry, but it's best to avoid suspicion."

"OK. I've had some thoughts of my own about this. Depends a bit on how your system is set up." He took off his backpack and pulled out a black box with several sockets and leads attached. Luke was pleased to see that it looked just like some anonymous piece of computer equipment, and would hardly be noticed in the rack of other gear. Hoa busied himself examining the set-up and attaching leads.

"There," he said, satisfied. "Now give me your phone. It's an Android device, you said? A Nexus? We'd be stuffed if it was an iPhone."

He fiddled with Luke's phone for a few minutes and installed a new app. "OK, you're good to

go," Hoa said.

At the start of the following day, the Christmas music was going strong as Mr Pando did the rounds of the counters. Mr Pando had found another copy of his original CD, it seemed, and the unenthusiastic singer was mechanically working through 'Oh Christmas Tree' again. She might as well have been singing a shopping list.

Luke couldn't help noticing how often Mr Pando found an opportunity to rest his hands on the shoulders, back or arms of the female workers as he did the rounds. Very touchy-feely. The women said that it was never quite enough to consitute harrassment, but it was close.

Finally, Pando headed out the door and back to his office. Luke picked up his phone and touched the new icon, then the controls which popped up. The Christmas carols faded gently away into silence. Immediately, there was a sense of relief among both staff and shoppers. Slumped shoulders lifted.

"Oh, good!" a lady at Luke's counter said, "it's stopped".

"That's brilliant," Mee Ying said, smiling broadly.

"Just make sure you give me a heads-up if you spot Pando back on the floor again and I'll crank it back up. And now for some fun..." He fiddled with his phone again.

"What are you doing now?"

"Something Hoa built in. Every ten minutes it's going to connect through to his speaker phone and play heavy metal music at him."

Mee Ying laughed, but put her hand on Luke's arm. "You'd better put the music on again, here comes Mr Pando's wife. She's sure to tell him if there's no music playing down here."

Mrs Pando came up to the counter. She was a severe-looking woman, in her middle fifties like her husband. Luke grabbed up his phone and hurriedly tapped at the controls in the special app.

Whether he missed the correct control or whether Hoa had wired things up wrongly, Luke never knew, but seconds later the audio system crackled and he was horrified to hear voices booming out over the crowded store. Mr Pando's voice. And that of one of the female secretaries.

"Just a little Christmas kiss, my dear," Pando was saying in a wheedling tone.

"No! No! Get away from me!" the young woman was saying. "Get your hands off..."

Luke stabbed frantically at his phone, and the voices faded into silence. Mrs Pando was staring up at the audio system. Her face was grim. She narrowed her eyes, firmed her shoulders, and headed off for the stairs.

"Whoops!" Luke said.

Heart of Oak

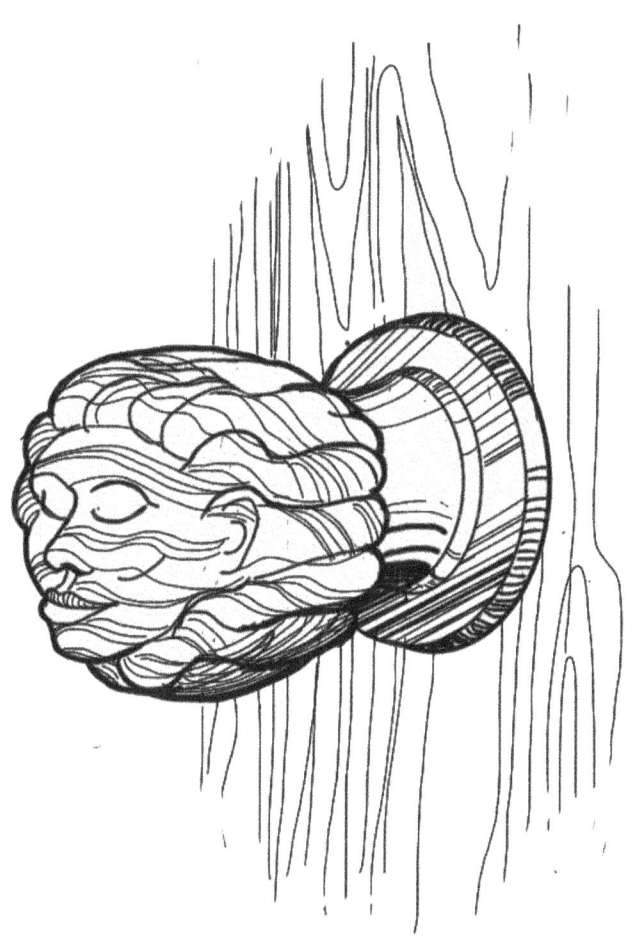

The street was a mess. The violent storm that had swept in the previous night had ripped up trees or broken off huge branches, torn off the roofs of several houses, and tossed rubble everywhere.

It was my job to fix it all up. I'm a team leader in the local State Emergency Service, and I was leading a group of volunteers to sort out the problems the storm had caused in this area. It was a Saturday morning. So much for the weekend.

We weren't doing full repairs, of course. Just helping out by stretching tarpaulins over the gaps in people's roofs, using chain-saws on the larger trees which had fallen into the street, clearing other debris and generally trying to make things safe. There were a dozen of us in the street, easy to spot by our bright orange work gear.

During the week I work as a tree surgeon, my own business. A pretty good background for an SES worker. I'm used to heights, and I know trees.

We were working our way slowly along the street and we'd reached the end. It was a dead-end street, and at the end was this big old two-storey house. Two-storey houses are pretty rare around here; or at least they used to be. These days you get a lot of two- or even three-storey McMansions popping up in the newer suburbs. But this was a long-established locality, and most of the houses were typical single-storey dwellings.

However, here at the end of the street was this really old place, two storeys high. It had probably been the original mansion for a rural property, built by some rich family owning all of the land around here, long ago sold off for sub-division. The house had seen better days, needed a couple of coats of paint at least. And now, after the storm, it was missing a lot of tiles from its roof.

My team had just come down from the roof of the house next door, and I collared Jim Bates, my assistant. "What about this place?" I asked, indicating the old mansion.

"Yeah, we rang the bell, but doesn't seem like there's anybody home," he said.

"There's a car in the driveway," I pointed out. A red Honda Civic, maybe ten years old.

"Yeah, well, what can I tell you? Nobody's answering the door." He shrugged and turned away. There was still a lot to do on the other side of the street.

I looked up at the building again. It didn't seem right just to leave it. I walked up the path and hammered on the door. Maybe the bell was broken. But there was still no reply. I walked around the side of the house as far as I could go, but there was a tall fence cutting off access. Topped with spikes, I now saw.

I decided to have a chat with the neighbours. They ought to know where the owner was. I went over to the house whose roof we'd just finished securing. The old couple who lived there were standing on their front porch, looking around at all the devastation.

At my question, the grey-haired man shook his head. "Haven't seen him today. That's the Archer boy. Keeps to himself, doesn't do any damned work around the house. Good-for-nothing, he is."

His wife, a pleasant-looking, plump woman, protested at this. "Oh, Gary, that's so unfair. You know what happened to him. And he's not a boy any more, he's a grown man. He has... Well, he *had* a perfectly good job until a couple of months ago."

The old man just shrugged. "Lost his job, though, didn't he? The school wouldn't keep him on. From what I hear, he spent half his time staring out of the window instead of teaching. Not that I think teaching kids about art is any kind of sensible job for a man."

"But you haven't seen him around today?" I asked, eager to stem this tide of gossip, which was none of my business. "Do you think he's away on holiday or something?"

"Him? No, he wouldn't be able to afford it. Besides, I heard him working in his back yard again last night, even though the storm was coming. All the lights on. He's been building something, I don't know what. Chopping and hammering till all hours.

A boat, or something, maybe, though why he'd want a boat I don't know."

"Well, he's not answering his door now. Perhaps he was hurt during the storm."

The old man nodded thoughtfully with a down-turned mouth. "Suppose it's possible. Come to think of it, I think there *is* a tree down next door."

The woman agreed, her face suddenly full of concern. "Yes, of course there is. That big oak tree, we can't see it any more. Oh dear, I do hope he's all right. I didn't think much of it, there are so many other trees down."

That settled it. I needed to do something about this. I left the couple talking and walked into the street to use my phone and call the police. I wasn't authorized to try to enter the house or the yard without permission, but the police could.

It was only a few minutes before a police vehicle pulled up. It can't have been far away. I guess they had been almost as busy in this area after the storm as we had been.

A young policeman climbed out. "Mr Bridges? I'm Constable Jackson. Tim Jackson. What's up?" I explained, and together we went up to the door of the old mansion.

Tim looked at the big old door sceptically. "We won't get that open in a hurry," he said. "Not without one of the rams the Drug Squad use. You sure he's at home?"

"Well, no, but his car's still here. And the folks next door reckon he was working in his back yard last night, before the storm hit."

Even as I said this, I could see the lady from next door bustling up, probably unwilling to miss out on any of the excitement.

"I'm Janet Ainsworth," she said to Tim, slightly out of breath from her rapid walk. "I'm Bobby Archer's next door neighbour. Oh, I shouldn't call him that. It's Robert Archer, of course. It's just that we've known him since he was a little boy."

"And you think he's still home?" asked the policeman.

"Well, I think so, yes. Oh dear, I'm so worried. It was awful what happened to him, just awful. He doesn't need any more grief in his life, poor man."

Tim Jackson glanced at me, but I just shook my head to show I didn't understand any more than he did. "What was that, Mrs Ainsworth?"

"Oh dear, didn't you know? It was in all the papers. Well, no, I suppose you wouldn't connect it, and you policemen must see terrible things like that every day, I suppose. How awful that must be for you."

"Mrs Ainsworth…"

"Oh, yes. Well, it was his wedding day, and there he was at the church, waiting for his bride. But there was a terrible accident, just terrible. There was a truck, it ran a red light. Well, they were all killed, the bride, I mean, and her father. Well, that was a year ago, and poor Bobby hasn't been the same ever since. I mean, who would be?"

All very interesting, no doubt, and tragic. But surely not very relevant to today. I was getting tired, and all I really wanted to do was to get on with the day's work and put a tarpaulin on this guy's roof to help him out. Maybe I should just leave it with the police. On the other hand, if there had been some kind of an accident then it was my job to help organise a rescue.

While I dithered, Tim stepped off the porch and started to examine the front windows, looking for a way in. I stayed, reluctantly, with Mrs Ainsworth. Suddenly she exclaimed. "Oh, look!" she said. "The doorknob!"

I looked where she was pointing. The large round wooden doorknob had been delicately carved to represent a human face. A woman's face. A beautiful young woman.

"Well, I never knew he'd done that," she said. "That's Elizabeth. His bride, you know. Isn't that lovely? He's an art and woodwork teacher, you know, and I believe he's exhibited some of his own work at a local gallery, though I never saw it."

Tim called out to us. "I've gotten this window open. I'll climb through and let you in." In a matter of a couple of minutes the three of us were standing in the hallway. Doubtless Tim should have dismissed Mrs Ainsworth at this point, as she had no excuse for entering the house, but instead we all stood there staring.

It was astonishing. Every exposed wooden surface had been carved: the panelling, the doorknobs, the banister of the staircase, and every rail. Wood chips from the carving were scattered all over the floor. Elizabeth's face was everywhere, carrying every expression of which a human face is capable, from grief to joy. And her naked body was depicted too, in smooth, beautiful, frankly erotic curves, twisted and elongated where necessary to fit the form of the wood.

The panelling had been carved in bas-relief into delicate wooden murals, showing Bobby Archer's lost bride in a variety of situations. Dancing, shopping, walking down the aisle, naked in bed. A nude young man – presumably Archer himself – appeared in one or two of these, coupling with the young woman. Mrs Ainsworth looked at these with her mouth open for a few moments, then gulped, muttered an excuse, and hurried off.

"Bloody hell," I said, and Tim Jackson nodded.

"Poor bastard," he said. Then he straightened up and returned to his duty. "What was his name again? Robert Archer?" He started forward, shouting: "Archer? Mr Archer? Are you home?"

We walked slowly through the rooms. Archer's obsession was everywhere. The kitchen was a fantasy of carving, every leg of the kitchen table shaped into a young woman's body, the table-top carved fantastically into yet more scenes of Elizabeth's life. The cupboards, the doors... No piece of wood seemed to have been left untouched. I had the feeling that if I opened a drawer and took out a box of matches, every match would have been carved into the shape of his lost love. Wood shavings were almost ankle deep here.

By the time we reached the back of the house, there had been no answer, and we could see out of the kitchen window that there was a tree blown over in the back yard. Dreading what we would find, we went out.

The oak tree was tipped far over to lie with its spreading roots lifted up into the air. It wasn't a particularly huge or old tree for an oak, and its trunk was perhaps a yard across. But the arborist in me could see that it had been dying long before the storm arrived, its upper leaves unseasonably brown. And I could see exactly why.

Robert Archer had been carving here, too. The lower trunk of the tree had been carved, while living, into the body of a nude young woman, her arms two outstretched branches. Her face had been carved into it, too. A screaming face. Elizabeth's face as perhaps it had looked in her last moment of terror before the truck hit her bridal car.

And pinned beneath the tree, in a final and fatal embrace with his beloved, was Robert Archer.

Coffee Spoons

Graham Peterson struggled with the door of his wardrobe. It was warped, and getting it open took more strength than he could spare these days.

With the wardrobe finally open, he reached in and took out his black suit. He examined it critically. The jacket wasn't too bad, but the pants were starting to become threadbare. He'd have to try to find a replacement pair at the Op Shop soon.

Standing at the mirror over the sink, he knotted his black tie. Even doing that was getting harder as the arthritis in his hands became worse.

Sighing, he picked up the tabloid newspaper. It was folded over to show the death and funeral notices, and he had circled two of the entries. He checked his watch. Still enough time.

Graham left the boarding house and walked the few yards to the bus stop. He had the route carefully planned out and, as always, had allowed plenty of time to get where he needed to go.

As it was, he reached the funeral parlour in plenty of time. Too much time, really. So he walked down the street and found a little park where he could sit for a while. It was pleasant to sit in the sun, warming up his old frame, until it was time to walk back.

Most of the mourners were there now. Someone handed him a memorial booklet. He went quietly in to the chapel and sat at the back. He put on his reading glasses and started to read carefully through the booklet, which briefly described the life of the deceased, Mark Barton. Died of a heart attack, just a few months into his retirement. What a poor reward for a life's work!

The service began with some sad classical music. A few minutes later, the celebrant stepped to the front, bowed slightly in respect to the flower-laden coffin and said a few anodyne words. There followed a video presentation which Mark's daughter had put together, giving a moving tribute to her father's life and his work as a mining engineer. Graham watched with genuine interest. Always interesting to find out about other people's lives.

Then came a sobbing attempt at a eulogy from Mark's widow. Graham thought it was a pity that the family had allowed their mother to try this. Eventually, her face red with weeping, she gave it up and sat down again.

Finally, the coffin was wheeled away and the mourners filed out of the chapel into the neighbouring reception room.

Graham headed directly for the counter where tea and coffee was being served. *I have measured out my life with coffee spoons*, he thought. T.S. Elliot had it right.

With coffee in hand he stood surveying the refreshments. It was nearly lunchtime now, and he was pleased to see a generous array of sandwiches, party pies and lamingtons. He loaded up a plate and went to sit down.

Mark's daughter was slowly circling the room and talking to the mourners.

"Hello," she said to Graham when she reached him. "I don't think we've met. How did you know Dad?"

Graham was ready. "I worked with him for a while when he was at BHP Headquarters here in Melbourne. He was a bit younger than me, but we always got on well together. When I saw his name in the paper, I thought I should come along, pay my respects. So sorry for your loss."

"Thank you," she said smiling, and moved on. Easy. It was harder when the widows talked to you, they knew too much.

He finished his plate of food, went back for another coffee and then visited the toilets. When he came out the mourners were dispersing.

He checked his watch. He would have to get a move on if he wasn't to be late to the funeral of Mrs Clarke. Sitting on the tram after using his discount pensioner travel card, he read through the death notices again.

Mrs Emily Clarke. Forty-three years old, died "after a long illness", it said in the paper. *Cancer then, such a pity*, he thought. Funeral at St Stephen's Church, followed by a private cremation. No flowers by request. Perfect, really.

He realised with a start that as yet he hadn't worked out how he knew Mrs Clarke. He was getting slack, he thought irritably, and started to consider. With that age difference, he could have been her teacher. But then, her maiden name wasn't given, and a teacher would be expected to know that. A neighbour, then. That would do.

He didn't want to skip the funeral. Yesterday he hadn't been able to find any suitable event to attend. He had to be careful. He tried to avoid names which didn't sound Anglo-Saxon, and of course, those which he would have needed a car to get to.

He had been doing this for several years now, ever since his meagre superannuation had run out and he had been forced to go on the government pension, which barely covered his rent and medication.

Graham felt he had built up a real expertise. There had been a couple of close calls, but pleading a bad memory was always helpful, and at his age, all too plausible.

St Stephen's was a pretty little church just off the main road of one of the inner suburbs. The small car park was already almost full. He checked his watch. The tram had been slow and he was quite late, so he hurried in and sat down quietly. The minister was already speaking.

Graham realised that he hadn't been given a memorial or order-of- service booklet, perhaps because he had been late. Oh well, he might be able to pick one up after the service and scan it quickly. In the meantime, he needed to pay attention.

Emily Clarke's sister Anne, a slim woman in her forties, gave a brief eulogy, mainly talking about her sister's courage in the last few years of her illness. Breast cancer, Graham deduced. Awful. So sad.

Though Graham had attended hundreds of funerals by now, he was not indifferent to the grief he saw almost every day. He often felt deeply moved by the struggles of the relatives to cope with their loss. It didn't overwhelm him, though. He had had plenty of his own grief over the years. Seeing others in a sad state somehow made him feel less alone. That was almost a religious feeling, he thought, though he no longer believed in God.

The service came to an end, and people started filing out. Would there be any refreshments? There hadn't been any mention of a reception during the ceremony. But he could see that people seemed to be turning towards the back of the church, not towards the street, and so he followed them. Ah, there was a small church hall behind the church.

Mrs Clarke's sister Anne was welcoming visitors as they entered the hall. He nodded to her, shook her hand, murmured his condolences. He expected her to let him pass by so that she could greet the next person, but instead she held his hand for a second longer than he expected and looked sharply at him for a moment. Then her gaze shifted, she released his hand and he went in.

There was a condolence book set up on a table just inside. Everyone was writing something in it, so he followed suit, writing his name and adding a generic expression of sympathy.

There was tea and coffee inside, biscuits and cake, and a fruit platter. Trying to achieve at least a semblance of a balanced diet, he took a few pieces of fruit along with two of the small cakes. He sat down next to a small table so he could rest his coffee and plate there.

He hadn't been there long when Anne came and sat down next to him.

"How did you know my sister?" she said, looking closely at him. Her voice was unfriendly. Graham began to have a bad feeling.

"Ah… I used to be a neighbour of hers. Lived a few houses down the street. I saw the name in the paper, thought…"

Anne interrupted him. "Where was that?"

Graham was struggling. "Um, it was here, not far from here… I…"

"How long ago?" she asked abruptly.

He felt himself beginning to tremble. "Oh, about five years ago, I think."

"You're a liar," she said grimly. "A bad liar. Emily and I grew up in Western Australia, spent most of our lives there. Emily only moved here to Melbourne last year to live with me when her cancer came back. Why are you *really* here?"

He felt himself blushing. Never mind, he could talk his way out of this. "Oh, how embarrassing. I must have made a mistake. Perhaps this Mrs Clarke isn't the one I knew." He tried to stand up to leave, but Anne gripped his arm tightly.

"Look at me," she said fiercely. "You are still lying. Tell me why you are really here. You *must* tell me."

Baffled, frightened by the intensity of this woman, he was truly embarrassed now. He had to tell the truth. "I... I came for the food," he said, ashamed. "I don't have much to live on now. I come to funerals for the tea and coffee and the refreshments. Oh, and to be with people, instead of being alone in my room." He was appalled to find that tears were dripping down his cheeks. He looked down, away from Anne's intense gaze, hating himself, hating his self-pity.

She relaxed her grip a little and put her other hand on his shoulder. When he regained his composure a little and lifted his gaze, he saw that she was looking at him less aggressively. Only then did he start to think that her face was somehow familiar to him.

"That's really true?" she asked, disbelief still in her voice. "That's really the only reason you are here?" He nodded, still unable to speak.

"I thought you had come here to make trouble," she said, shaking her head and was silent for a while. "I thought I recognised you, and then I read your name in the condolence book. You *are* Graham Peterson, aren't you?" He nodded, still baffled.

She was silent again. "Listen to me," she said at last. "I was born Samantha Anne Peterson. But I hated being called 'Sam', so I started using my middle name. My sister was Emily. Samantha and Emily Peterson, that's what we were called as kids. And my father's name was Graham."

"No, no," he said, panic rising, half-rising to flee. It was another life she was talking about. A life which had happened to someone who vanished long ago. A life too painful to recall. "No, you must be mistaken. I don't want..." But as he gazed into Anne's face, he began to recognise the child that she had been when he saw her last, nearly forty years ago. He sat back down.

"Samantha..." he said at last. Then, with a sudden shock: "And Emily... Oh God! Emily is *dead*." Dead, his own child. He had attended her funeral, all unknowing. He put his face in his hands and began to sob.

After a long while, he forced himself to stop. "She wouldn't let me see you," he said in a hoarse voice. "Your mother. Told the court I was violent, bashed her. That I was an abusive father. She got full custody. No visiting rights. They let that happen in those days. Took you both off to the other side of the country. Even if I'd been allowed to visit, I could never have afforded to come."

Anne looked at him steadily. "And were you? Violent? Abusive?"

He shook his head. "I swear to God. I only ever hit your mother once, slapped her, once in all our life together. I was sorry straight afterwards, and I told her so. That was the only time, but she never forgave me. Do you remember ever seeing me hit her? Or hurting you or Emily? *Do* you?" Now he was being fierce in his turn.

"No," she said quietly, "I don't remember that. Mum was... well, she *was* pretty hard to live with most of the time. She really hated you, I'm not really sure why. She was a bit unbalanced about it, to be honest. I had a photo of you, me sitting on your knee... I had to hide it from her, she tore up all the others."

"It was probably my fault. I was always working too hard at the office. We had arguments all the time. I started to work even longer and longer hours at work, just to keep out of her way. So it got worse and worse."

They were both silent for a very long time. Then Anne looked down at her hands. "Look," she said, and paused again. "I suppose in a fairy tale I would throw my arms around you, tell you I'd been trying to find you all my life, and invite you to come and live me with me. But..."

He shook his head sadly. "No. We are just strangers now. I couldn't be anything other than a burden to you. I'm sure you don't need that. I had better go." This time she let him stand.

Anne looked up at him, tears now in her own eyes. "Today has been... just too much, too much. Losing Emily. And then you being here... I can't come to terms with it all, not all on one day. You'll have to give me time."

"I understand," he said. Then, after a pause: "I loved you both, very much," he said, with a catch in his throat. "A long time ago."

She nodded slowly. Then, fumbling in her handbag, she said: "Listen, I'll give you my card. I run my own business, a travel agency. Give me a call in a few days, perhaps we can talk again."

He took the card, limped outside and walked off. When he reached the main street a few minutes later, a tram was just coming.

On board the tram, Graham sat holding Anne's card in the palm of his hand. He hadn't yet looked at it, didn't know the name of her business, or where it was located. He realised that there were so many things he didn't know, questions he hadn't asked. Was Anne married? Did she have children, his grandchildren? They could have been there at the funeral and he would not have known.

No, he decided at last. He had no right to know about Anne's life, no right to interfere now, no right to suddenly become a burden to this stranger.

There was a container for used tickets on the wall near to him. Just before he reached his stop, he reached over and slid the card into it.

Storytellers

The bus seemed to be taking forever that morning. Mary Benson fumed as she craned her neck past the others in the queue. She was going to be late for her shift at the hospital. At least she was on a normal day shift for the moment. She hated the evening shift in the Emergency Department when you had so many more drunks, drug abusers and car accident victims to deal with at the counter. Thank God for the security window, though that didn't stop the verbal abuse.

Here came the bus at last. But as usual, it was nearly full already, and she would have to cram in and stand.

Just as she started to climb up the stairs, though, someone seemed to stumble into her from behind and she felt a hand slap onto her right buttock and squeeze. Flushing, she turned to see who had assaulted her, but the other passengers were pushing her forward onto the bus. To her right, a young man with a stubble beard forced his way up, and then deeper into the bus. Behind her, a short balding man in a grey suit climbed on, deliberately looking away from her. Once on board, he turned his back on her. Him, then! What a creep!

Mary briefly debated making a scene, but thought better of it. But she kept her eye on the man. If he tried to grope another woman -- there was a tall young woman with closely cropped hair on the other side of him -- she would punch him. Nothing he could say or do would shock her. She saw and heard far worse almost every day in her job.

-:-

Bob Graham had been thinking about his upcoming meeting that morning with the sales manager, and he wasn't looking forward to it. It had been a bad quarter, sales were down. It was only to be expected. There was a new model coming out next month and their chairman had been raving in public about how good it was going to be. Of course customers were deferring their purchases. Why buy an old one now when a better one was just about to hit the stores? But there was no use telling his hot new manager that. He kept piling on the pressure, wanted to clear the inventory. Bob was ten years older than his manager. It was humiliating, but he had to keep biting his tongue instead of telling the guy what a fool he was.

Finally, the bus arrived. Just in front of him was a thin middle-aged woman dressed in a black outfit with white trim. Her face was severe. Looked like a school-teacher maybe, a tough one. He'd had a few of those when he was a kid, what seemed like a century ago.

As the doors of the bus opened, the woman started to climb the stairs and Bob began to follow. Just at that moment, a scruffy young man bounded forward, trying to jump the queue, it seemed, and knocked into Bob so heavily that he lost his balance and stumbled forward. Encumbered by the briefcase in his right hand, Bob flailed out with his left to stop himself falling, and found to his intense embarrassment that he had put his hand on the woman's rump. He was forced to push briefly on her to regain his balance, though now the young man was helping, pulling him up by his jacket.

"Sorry, mate," said the scruffy man, and then bounded up the stairs.

There were more passengers behind Bob, all pushing to get on the bus before the doors closed, complaining about the delay. So he climbed up. Should he apologise to the woman? No, his explanation would seem like a feeble excuse, and she wouldn't believe him. He turned away from her at the top of the stairs to hide his embarrassment.

He glared across at the young man, who had incredibly just gained a seat, as the elderly lady in front of him was getting up, probably to get off at the next stop. There was no justice in the world. Probably one of those unemployed louts heading in to that stupid Occupy protest. Why couldn't he grow up and get himself a job?

-:-

Shaun O'Brien smiled as he sat down, pushing in to get the old woman's seat the instant she stood up. He ignored the glares from the other nearby passengers who'd been on the bus longer than him. They could all get stuffed, he didn't give a flying fuck what they thought.

He felt in his jacket pocket for the old guy's wallet. Stupid prick had been a pushover, literally. He laughed inwardly, thinking about the face on that uptight bitch when the old guy had put his hand on her bum. What she needed was a good fuck, that would cheer her up. Probably some kind of secretary, he thought idly. But not the kind that would sit on the boss' knee.

He wondered how much cash was in the old guy's wallet. People didn't carry so much cash these days. He'd have to move quick to make what he could from the credit cards. Maybe he could sell the driver's license and other ID. Identity theft was a big deal these days, they said, but Shaun wasn't sure that he knew the right contacts yet. Maybe one of the guys at the factory could give him a tip. He would ask Jacko tomorrow, when he went back to work.

He glanced up. Standing in front of him in jeans and T-shirt was a good-looking young chick, with short cropped hair. The T-shirt read *A Woman Needs a Man Like a Fish Needs a Bicycle*, with a cartoon of a goldfish on a push-bike seat. What the crap did that mean? Nice tits, though. He wondered what she'd say if he asked her out. Mind you, he'd nicked the seat from her, so she'd probably be pretty snarky. As if to confirm that, she looked down suddenly and glared at him.

-:-

Jen Petridis stared down in anger at the bastard who'd pushed past everyone else to get the seat. Selfish prick! Jen didn't care about the seat herself, but the woman next to her was in the later stages of pregnancy, anyone could tell. Except this jerk.

She took her attention away from him, it wasn't worth the angst. She started thinking again about the software she was writing, part of a multi-media simulation game for the Museum. If only they wouldn't keep changing their minds about their requirements! It was starting to cost her firm a lot of money they hadn't budgeted for, and the Museum was trying to argue that their changes weren't variations to the contract. Still, that wasn't really her concern, that was her boss' worry. Instead, she started to plot out the class structure she would need to simulate the dinosaur population in the game.

After a while, she glanced again at the pregnant woman next to her. She was very neatly dressed, but the poor woman looked ill and tired. Probably an immigrant from Eastern Europe, working in some sweat-shop, sewing clothes together for a pittance per piece. What a lousy job that would be, particularly if you were pregnant, maybe coping with morning sickness. Catch that ever happening to Jen! Her girlfriend and she had decided some time ago that they wouldn't try for kids. All that IVF stuff was way too hard and expensive.

-:-

Lena Balodis was nervous, and her feet hurt. She wished that the scruffy man hadn't taken the seat. Still, it wasn't far now to her stop. Thank goodness she could sit down most of the day there. Being a personal assistant to the manager was challenging, but he was a good man and tried to make it easier for her now she was expecting, reduce the running around. The firm had a pretty good maternity leave scheme, too.

But her gaze kept drifting back to the dark-skinned youth, not much older than a teenager, who had been standing in the corner ever since she had got onto the bus. He looked as though he might be a Pakistani, and he was wearing a bulky backpack, which he kept fiddling with, adjusting it on his shoulders. He had a grim, unhappy expression.

Lena had been on holiday in London in July 2005, when terrorists blew up three trains on the Underground and then a double-decker bus. Though she had been nowhere near the incidents, they had made a powerful impression on her. Ever since then, she had kept a worried eye on other passengers when she travelled on public transport. Especially now when she was carrying her first baby inside her.

The youth kept looking at his watch. Was there some pre-arranged plan, some scheme to blow up their explosives simultaneously?

She didn't know what to do, but felt the stirrings of panic. Should she try and tell someone else? Talk to the youth and plead with him not to do it? But he might set it off as soon as she spoke to him. All it seemed she could do was pray, and so she did.

The bus pulled in to its next stop. It was Lena's stop, and she struggled through the crush to reach the doorway. Fortunately, it was a popular destination, and many other people were getting off, so it wasn't too hard. Lena stepped down to the pavement with a sigh of relief and started to walk towards her office.

But then, for some reason, she turned and looked back.

In horror, she saw that the dark young man was following her, and now he was taking off his backpack, starting to fumble with its zips. She stood, frozen with terror, as he approached.

-:-

Asanka Weerasinghe gave a puzzled look at the pregnant lady as he passed her. She was white-faced, slightly green, maybe she was going to be sick? Asanka didn't know what he could do about that, so he kept on walking, his heavy pack now carried in his hands.

His shoulders were aching painfully with carrying the weight on his back. The straps aren't adjusted properly, he thought, or maybe he should just have bought a better pack. Actually, he thought, the real problem was how much weight he was carrying in there, too much stuff. It hadn't helped that he'd had to stand the whole way on the bus.

He glanced at his watch again. Was there still time? Yes.

There was a coffee shop here. It was crowded, but he went in, seeing a small vacant table and chair near the window. He set the heavy pack down on the table gratefully and sat down.

He unzipped the backpack, took out the laptop computer from among the heavy text-books, opened it up, and started to type. There was still plenty of time before his creative writing class.

Life was full of stories, it seemed to him.

Acknowledgements

Many thanks to Robert Brunton, who has been unfailing in his encouragement of my writing efforts. Without his keen readership and support I think that my renewed interest in writing fiction might well have faltered.

Bob has also been kind enough to supply all of the charming interior illustrations for this book, which I feel greatly enhance its appeal.

Thanks also to my lovely wife Sue, without whose help I could do nothing.

About the Author

David Grigg is a retired software developer who lives in Melbourne, Australia. He worked in the field of interactive multimedia for over two decades, and has also worked in public relations and as a journalist and sub-editor. He is married, with one grown-up daughter and two grand-children.

Born in the north of England, he emigrated to Australia with his parents at the age of 13. He has lived in Australia ever since.

During the 1970s and 1980s, David was deeply involved in the science fiction fan community in Australia, publishing fanzines and helping organize SF conventions, eventually becoming Chairman of the 43rd World SF Convention held in Melbourne in 1985.

He is the author of a number of professionally published short stories and two short fantasy novels for teens, "Halfway House" and "Shadows".

Rightword

Editing, proofing, book design and publication services

*Your new book is your baby; it's precious to you. We understand that.
Let us help you to deliver it safe and well into the hands of your readers.*

Rightword offers a range of services to help you put your book together:

Copy-editing; proof-reading; typesetting and formatting; book design and layout; cover design; ebook production; assistance in working with printers and retailers.

For more information and to see samples of our work, please visit our website at *www.rightword.com.au*, or send an email to *book.publishing@rightword.com.au*.